FORTUNE OF THE WITCH

WITCHES OF KEATING HOLLOW
BOOK FIFTEEN

DEANNA CHASE

ABOUT THIS BOOK

Medium Harlow Thane has given up her life as a celebrity paranormal investigator. After her life was turned upside down by a devious and illusive ghost, all she wants is to settle down in Keating Hollow, running the new pub in town. Unfortunately for her, no matter how much she wants to give up ghost hunting, the ghosts won't quit her. Neither will her ex Cash Moses. With a ghost she just can't seem to banish and her ex hell-bent on righting the past, it looks like Harlow's plan for a quiet life isn't in the cards.

Cash Moses wants two things: revenge against the ghost who stole everything from him and Harlow Thane. In order to track down and eradicate the ghost, he needs Harlow's help, except she's not interested. Not in the ghost and not in him... or so she says. Somehow, he needs to find a way to get past her defenses so they can move on from their past and finally get their happily-ever-after.

CHAPTER 1

"Two Irish coffees, please," Brian Knox said, giving Harlow his devastatingly handsome smile.

"Seriously?" Shannon asked. His gorgeous red-headed wife was standing next to him. "You don't think we've had enough?"

"You said you wanted coffee." He grabbed her around the waist and nuzzled in to kiss her on her neck. "What else was I supposed to order?"

Laughing, she pretended to squirm away before finally melting into him. "Probably would have been best to get anything that doesn't have alcohol in it."

"But it's a celebration. Where's the fun in that?" He dislodged himself from her and gave Harlow a wink.

"Can't argue with that," Harlow said, already getting to work on brewing a fresh pot of coffee. It was the spring equinox, just after eight p.m., and the party in the town of Keating Hollow had been going on all day. It had started with a spring festival, followed by a group cleansing in the river, and now those who hadn't wanted the party to end had descended on Equinox, the new pub and music venue that Chad Garber had opened recently. Chad and his wife Hope had left about an hour ago, leaving Harlow in charge.

As long as there wasn't a sudden influx of patrons, Harlow was confident that she and Cam, the young man they'd hired a few months ago, could manage just fine.

He's hot, the resident ghost said into Harlow's ear.

"He's married," she said automatically, forgetting that she usually just ignored the spirit.

Not him. The one who just walked in.

Harlow gave a passing glance at the door and then did a double take.

I told you he was hot, the ghost said.

The ghost wasn't wrong. The first time Harlow had ever laid eyes on Cash Moses, she'd known then and there that she was a goner. Not only was he tall, dark, and handsome, but he was also full of life. He was the kind of man who just lit up a room. And it had been that vitality, more than anything else, that had caused her to spend the next ten years of her life being his ride or die. He hadn't just been her best friend; he'd also been her professional partner and the love of her life.

But that had all changed last year when she'd walked away from everything she'd built... including her relationship with Cash.

Harlow stifled a groan and cut her gaze away, pretending she hadn't noticed him. Maybe if she ignored him, he'd get the hint and go away. Not that he'd ever done that in the three months since he'd shown up in Keating Hollow and started randomly dropping in on her at Equinox.

No such luck.

"Harlow," he said as he sauntered up to the bar, that sexy half smile claiming his lips.

"Cash," she said with a sigh. "I told you I'm not interested."

"I heard you." He took a seat at the bar and said, "I'm here for a beer. Whatever you recommend that's on tap. You know what I like."

That was certainly true. She walked over to the taps, grabbed a chilled glass, and poured a porter from the Keating Hollow Brewery. Without a word, she placed it in front of him and then moved to the other end of the bar to serve Wanda Danvers, the local real estate agent, and her life partner, Cameron Copeland, who was also Miranda Moon's writing partner. Since Cameron, Miranda, and her husband, Gideon Alexander, had opened Mystic Road Studios, a new production company next to the pub, Harlow had gotten to know both couples fairly well, as they'd become frequent patrons of Equinox.

Wanda placed a set of keys on the bar and grinned at Harlow. "The owner of that house you applied to rent signed the papers today. I hope you're ready to move in."

"Seriously?" Harlow snatched up the keys and deposited them into the front pocket of her jeans. Ever since she'd moved to town, she'd been renting a tiny studio apartment above a garage, just waiting for something perfect to come along for her to rent. It was notoriously hard to find decent rentals in the quaint witchy town. And even harder to buy anything. Most people ended up buying raw land and building when they wanted to settle permanently in Keating Hollow. "I thought for sure they were going to rent it to that couple that showed up after we took a look at it."

"They wanted to do month to month. Since you were willing to sign a two-year lease, you won." Wanda winked at her. "Told you that would work. The owner is tired of turnover renters."

"Then thanks for the tip, because I have no interest in going anywhere for the foreseeable future." Harlow got them their drinks, and when Shannon took a seat next to Wanda, Harlow asked, "Can I get you another Irish coffee?"

"I better not," she slurred slightly and then giggled. "If I have anything else, I might have to be carried out of here."

Harlow chuckled to herself and nodded. "It's good to know your limits."

"Shannon!" Brian called from across the room. "You've got to try these chocolate-covered caramels." He reached into a white paper bag and pulled out one of the chocolates.

"Oh, that's exactly what I need." Shannon stood, pointed at him, and flicked her wrist as she sent a bolt of her air magic in his direction. Multiple things happened at once. The magic hit Brian in the shoulder, sending him stumbling to the side as the magic whooshed past him and blasted the front door open.

"No!" Shannon cried when Brian dropped the chocolate, and she sent another bolt of magic to catch the sweet treat before it fell to the floor. The chocolate-covered caramel sailed smoothly right into Shannon's hand, and she held it up triumphantly as if she'd just won a jackpot.

The entire bar erupted in applause as they all hollered their approval.

Everyone except Harlow. The hair on the back of her neck stood up, and her skin had started to tingle the moment the door had swung open. Harlow instinctively reached into her torn left pocket, grabbed the iron spike she kept strapped to her thigh, and rushed out from behind the bar toward Brian.

The man was on one knee, holding his head with one hand while waving the other as if trying to shoo someone—or something—away. To those who didn't have medium abilities, it likely looked as though he was having some sort of fit. But Harlow knew better.

She grabbed Brian's hand and hauled him toward the wall. As soon as his back hit the sheetrock, she raised her arm and stabbed the ghost clinging to him through the chest, nailing him to the wall with her iron spike. The spirit let out a low growl, jerked as if trying to dislodge himself from the spike, and then disappeared into thin air with a loud *pop*.

The entire bar had gone silent except for the slow clapping that she knew had to be coming from Cash Moses.

"Well done, Harlow," he said from behind her. "It's good to see that even after taking a year off, your skills are still just as sharp as ever."

Harlow let out a long breath and ignored her ex just like she had for the past three months. Initially, he hadn't taken the news that she was giving up ghost hunting well and had showed up six months ago, asking her to get back into it. She'd considered it for about half a minute before shutting him down. She was done with willfully going after ghosts. It was too dangerous. She turned her gaze to Brian. "Are you all right?"

He blinked at her. "I think so. What the hell just happened?"

Shannon appeared by his side, her brow furrowed with concern. She pressed her hand to his cheek, her gaze scanning him as if to check for injuries. Then she turned to Harlow with her eyes narrowed slightly.

Harlow could feel the distrust streaming off the other witch, and she suppressed an exhausted sigh. This wasn't at all how she'd envisioned her day going when she'd woken up that morning, though she didn't know why she was so surprised. It was the spring equinox, one of the days when the veil separating the living and the shadow world was thinner. Spirit activity was to be expected on such a day. But for some reason, she'd deluded herself into believing that Keating Hollow might be different. She'd hoped the magic that seemed to be woven throughout the town would somehow repel the ghosts that were drawn to her during the solstice and that they'd have a harder time materializing.

So much for that theory.

Harlow yanked her spike out of the wall and then cleared her throat. "A spirit came through the door when Shannon's air magic caused it to burst open and immediately attached himself to you."

Shannon let out a gasp and covered her mouth with her hand, her eyes wide.

"What?" Brian glanced around, looking confused. "How? Why?"

"I don't know why, but the how is fairly easy. The veil between this world and the shadow world is very thin today," Harlow said. "It's easier for spirits to materialize." She left out the part about how she seemed to be some sort of magnet who gave them energy and then continued. "He could have been a spirit you've known either in this life or a past life, or he might have just been attracted to your energy."

"But since Harlow already sent him back to the shadow world," Cash said casually, "there's no way to know unless he materializes again. Then maybe we can ask some questions."

"Questions?" Shannon asked. "That thing is going to come back?"

Harlow eyed Shannon. "You saw him?"

A shudder ran through her as she nodded. "He was kinda greenish-gray. Like some sort of translucent gutter creature."

"Yeah, he did sort of look like that," Harlow said with a nod. "But it's highly unlikely he'll be back today. Not after I staked him with my spike. There's probably nothing to worry about."

Cash raised a skeptical eyebrow at her, and she suppressed

a wince. Now that a spirit had entered the bar on the equinox, it was likely that more would follow. It was as if a spiritual trail had been laid that would lead any restless souls right to Harlow.

"But…" Harlow said, rubbing the back of her neck. "Just to be safe, I think we'd better close up so I can do a cleansing. You know, better safe than sorry."

A couple of people groaned in disappointment.

Cam called out, "All right, everyone. You heard the boss. Time to settle up." He moved down the bar, handing out tickets.

In no time at all, most of the patrons had paid and filed out, wishing Harlow success with the cleansing. In addition to Cam, Harlow, and Cash, only Miranda and Gideon, Wanda and Cameron, and Shannon and Brian remained.

Miranda touched Harlow's arm. "How can we help?"

Harlow glanced at Cash and then back at Miranda. "Thank you, but Cash and I can handle the pub. The best thing for you guys to do is sage your homes when you get there. That will keep your energy clear of anyone uninvited through the night."

Miranda hesitated, and Harlow knew she wanted to argue, but when Shannon said, "Miranda, can you and Gideon give me and Brian a ride home? I don't think either of us should be driving."

"Of course," Miranda said and squeezed Harlow's hand. She leaned into Harlow and said, "Don't hesitate to call if you need anything. I can help."

Harlow nodded. "Thanks."

When they were gone, Harlow turned to Cam. "You can take off, too."

Cam glanced at Cash and frowned. "Nah. I'll stay to clean up unless I'll be in the way."

"No, it's not that," Harlow said. "It's just that... Well, sometimes unusual things can happen during an active cleansing."

His gaze cut to Cash again. "I bet." Then he finished wiping down the counter before heading for the door. "Just call if you need me to come back. I mean it."

"Thanks, but I'm sure I'll be fine," Harlow said and waved as he took off for the night.

Cash chuckled softly. "He's more worried about me than any stray spirits you might encounter."

"I know," Harlow snapped, not sure why she was taking her frustration out on him. It wasn't like he called the ghost. If he had, it would have latched onto him instead of the first warm body that got in its path.

Cash held his hands up. "No need to bark at me. I'm just here to help."

Harlow wanted to tell him to go, that she had this handled, but she knew that was reckless. Now that the veil was open, she needed backup. And Cash Moses was the best person for the job. "All right then. Let's get started before that spirit next to you manages to strip you naked."

"What?" He glanced from side to side, his lips curved down into a frown. When he didn't see any spirits, he looked down at his now almost completely unbuttoned shirt and swore under his breath. "She's back?" he asked Harlow, knowing she had a gift that usually allowed her see spirits before they materialized for everyone else.

"She's back," Harlow confirmed. Then she raised her spike over her head and lunged for Cash's ghostly stalker.

CHAPTER 2

*C*ash moved just before Harlow drove her spike right
through his left shoulder. He knew instantly that
Harlow had been going after the spirit he'd named Stella. It
was hard to miss when Stella was grabbing his ass. He yanked
his iron chain out of his pocket and spun on one heel.

Jackpot. He felt the chain wrap around the still-invisible
spirit, securing her in place. It took a few moments, but soon
enough the spirit materialized and shot daggers at Harlow
with her wide, sunken eyes.

"He's mine," Stella hissed, thrashing about but not quite
able to free herself from the iron.

Harlow let out a very put-upon sigh and walked up to the
ghost.

Stella glared at her. "Stay away from my man."

Harlow ignored her and looked at Cash. "Is this the real
reason you came to find me?"

"No," he said adamantly, wishing he could throttle Stella.
The ghost had been obsessed with him for a couple of months
now and always seemed to show up at the most inopportune

times. He'd eradicated her from his life over a dozen times, but nothing he did seemed to stick for very long. He was starting to think someone had cursed him to never be rid of her. "But I have to admit that if you manage to banish her, it's going to be an excellent perk."

"You weren't able to?" Harlow asked, tilting her head to study him.

"Obviously not. At least not permanently." He waved at Stella, who would likely break free of her restraints any moment. "Want to get on with it, or are you hoping you get another chance to aim that spike at me?"

Harlow rolled her eyes. "Don't be so dramatic. I wouldn't—"

Stella threw her arms up, breaking the hold the iron chain had on her, and then went straight for Cash.

He instantly put his arms up as if to shield himself. It was a rookie move, but she'd already broken his favorite ghost-hunting tool. The iron chain had served him for many years, trapping ghosts so that Harlow could banish them. Though the past year, he'd had to do his own banishings. And while he usually managed it, some of the banished spirits didn't take it kindly. He'd been haunted by more than his share of pissed-off ghosts recently.

Stella was different though. She wasn't mad; she was just persistent. For some reason, she seemed to think that if she tried hard enough, Cash would agree to be her boyfriend. Never mind that she was a ghost and completely out of touch with reality.

Harlow sprang into action, her skills just as sharp as they had been a year ago before she'd walked away from ghost hunting. In seconds, she had the ghost pressed up against the bar and the iron spike through her hip, pinning her to the wood structure. She glanced at Cash. "Do I need to question her?"

Sometimes ghosts only hung around until they delivered a message. In those cases, just listening to them was sometimes enough to get them to cross over. This wasn't one of those times.

"No. She doesn't have any unfinished business. She just refuses to cut ties with this world," Cash said.

"It looks more like she's refusing to cut ties with you," Harlow said, eyeing the ghost.

Stella was staring at Cash, her expression filled with longing. She met Cash's gaze and licked her pouty lips. "I could make you happy. All you have to do is give me a chance."

"Send her away, please," Cash begged Harlow.

Harlow smirked, and for a moment Cash thought that she might not grant his request. He envisioned the ghost sitting with him at the dinner table, tagging along on a hike, lying next to him in his bed, invading his shower... A shudder ran through him, and he made a face.

"You know I wouldn't do that to you," Harlow said, apparently reading his mind. In one swift motion, she grabbed her spike again, twisted, and called, "*Eicere!*"

Magic coated her hand and shot into her spike.

Stella's mouth formed a wide *O* as her eyes widened, and then suddenly the spirit shattered into a million pieces before fading into nothing.

"Thank you," Cash said, sitting on one of the barstools as he let out a sigh of relief. "I'm not going to miss that one."

"Where'd you find her?" Harlow's lips twitched into a tiny smile. "666-STALKER?"

"Cute." Cash chuckled. Gods, he'd missed working together. Missed her and their easy rapport. He was just about to tell her that when she crossed her arms over her chest and stared him down.

"I know what you're thinking," she accused, all of her humor gone. "The answer is still no. Especially since we both know that while you might want to work with me again, you're here in Keating Hollow because of that harlot who wouldn't leave you alone. Don't tell me that you wouldn't have throttled her if you'd had the opportunity."

Cash stared at her for a long moment. Harlow was wrong. He was in Keating Hollow because he'd inherited his aunt's home. It wasn't even until after he'd come to settle the estate that he'd realized she was in town. But he hadn't told her that. He didn't even know why. Instead, he'd tried to coax her into partnering with him again. She flatly refused, and he'd reluctantly let it go. But he hadn't been able to move on from her. And he knew he never would. He stood and walked over to her.

Harlow blinked up at him with her suspicious brown eyes. "What are you doing, Cash?"

He didn't answer. Instead, he pressed his palm to her cheek and caressed the bone lightly with his thumb.

Her eyes drifted closed as she leaned into his touch, and Cash knew right then and there that she wasn't over him. She might have left him and kept pushing him away, but it wasn't because she didn't want him. No. She absolutely did. That much was clear. He just needed to figure out how to help her heal from the past, and then maybe, just maybe, they could put their relationship back together.

"Showing you that not everything is about that ghost," he said softly. That much was true. He hadn't intended on staying in Keating Hollow. Not until he'd realized she'd made it her new home and that decision had nothing to do with the spirit.

Her eyes snapped open, and she took a step back. She averted her gaze and said, "It's getting late. I think you should probably go now."

"No," he said mildly, knowing that would get a rise out of her.

"No? You're joking, right?" She was staring at him, her expression incredulous. "What makes you think you can just walk in here and do whatever the hell you want?"

"I'm not doing whatever the hell I want," he said patiently. "I'm just refusing to leave because we both know that the closer it gets to midnight the easier it is for spirits to appear in our world. And since it seems this building is some sort of magnet for them, I'm not leaving you here by yourself."

Her jaw tensed, but she didn't argue the point. Instead, she said, "It's not usually like this. In fact, the winter solstice and New Year's Eve were tame. I think there was just so much magic in the air today that was exacerbated by the reverie, and all that energy is probably calling to them. Any spirit that's been wanting to materialize has been taking their chance."

"That's why I'm staying until you close up," Cash said as he grabbed a rag to start wiping down tables.

"You don't have to do that," Harlow said, reaching for the rag.

Cash took a step back as he hid the rag behind his back. "I know I don't have to. I want to. Now just relax and let me help you, Harlow. It's not a big deal."

She nodded, but they both knew it was, in fact, a big deal. Because today, after three hundred and seventy-eight days, Harlow Thane had let Cash Moses back into her life even if it was only for an evening.

He'd take it.

Forty-five minutes later, once the entire bar had been

wiped down, swept, and mopped, they did a thorough sage cleansing.

"I hope that does the trick," Harlow muttered as she and Cash walked out the front door.

He waited while she locked up and then stood there with his hands in his pockets, unable to physically make himself leave her side.

"I've got it from here," Harlow said, tucking her keys into her small bag that was draped across her body.

"I'll walk you to your car," Cash said, pressing his hand to the small of her back. Harlow opened her mouth to protest, but Cash cut her off. "Just let me do this, okay? I want to make sure you're safe. Just be glad I'm not insisting on taking you home." Though he really wanted to. If he had his way, he'd tuck her into his Jeep, take her back to his great-aunt's house, and tuck her into his bed where he could keep an eye on her until the equinox was over. But he knew better than anyone that she'd never agree to that.

Harlow laughed. "Okay, Cash. You can walk me to my car. Just this once."

"Thank you." He glanced down the cobblestone street, looking for her car, but he didn't see it. "Where's the Mustang?"

"Gone," she said with a sigh.

He paused and stared down at her. "You sold the Mustang?"

"To my sister," she said with a shrug. "It wasn't practical for driving around here in the winter, and she needed a new set of wheels, so... It was better to keep it in the family, right?"

"I guess," he said, feeling a pang of loss. Even though he hadn't seen the car since he'd been in town, it hadn't occurred to him that she'd have let it go. He'd assumed it was parked somewhere other than on Main Street or she'd gotten another vehicle and kept it at home in a garage. How many memories did he and Harlow have in that 1965 Mustang? There were so many burned into his brain. Their first date. First kiss. First... everything. It was also where he'd asked her to marry him and where she'd broken off their engagement just a year earlier. That memory was a punch in the gut. He reached into his pocket and ran his fingers over the small velvet box that held the engagement ring he kept with him at all times. He didn't know why. He just knew he always had to have it near him.

At least Imogen had the Mustang now. Though he was skeptical that she'd keep it maintained the way Harlow had. She'd treated that car as if it were a precious treasure. As far as Cash was concerned, it was.

"Where's Imogen now?" he asked. Because Harlow had kept him at arm's length the past three months, they hadn't caught up on anything personal. He hadn't even told her about inheriting his aunt's house. He wondered if she knew and just never said anything about it. Or if she was just doing her best not to think about him at all.

"The Napa Valley," she said, sounding tired. "She's working at a winery, handling their weddings."

"That's good." He glanced at her face and saw the raw pain there. Taking her hand in his, he squeezed it. "She'll come around... eventually."

"Maybe. Maybe not." As they approached a Subaru Crosstrek, Harlow turned to him. "Thanks for your help tonight. Though I'm not sure I would have needed it if you hadn't stepped into the pub."

He chuckled because it was true. He'd been the one who'd attracted the ghost she'd had to banish. And while she'd had to deal with another one, it's not like Cash had done much of anything to help her. She'd have been fine on her own. "It wasn't worth the risk leaving you alone in the pub. We both know that having two people present instead of one can be enough to keep spirits away."

"That and the sage from the cleansing," she quipped.

"You're enjoying busting my balls, aren't you?" he asked, once again amused.

"Always." She paused for just a second, then she pressed up onto her tiptoes and gave him a ghost of a kiss on his cheek. "Thank you again. Goodnight, Cash."

"Night, Harlow. Don't hesitate to call me if anything or anyone pops up."

She gave him a quick nod and then climbed into her small SUV.

Cash stood on the street for a few minutes, waiting until she backed out and then disappeared into the night. It took everything he had not to jump into his Jeep and follow her home. He rubbed at his chest, right where the ache remained from his heartbreak just over a year ago. But when the area didn't pulse beneath his fingers, he realized that finally, after twelve months of aching for Harlow, the pain had started to fade.

It had happened when she'd kissed him.

Now all he needed to do was give her a reason to do it again.

CHAPTER 3

hat in the hell was I doing, Harlow thought as she sped away from downtown. Away from Cash Moses.

She'd let him get in her head. She'd enjoyed spending time with him too much. Hell, she'd even kissed him.

That was *not* in the plan.

The evening had just felt so *familiar.* She and Cash fending off zealous spirits together had been such a part of the life they'd shared for ten years that when they'd needed to, stepping right back into those rolls had been second-nature. And the only time in the past year when she'd actually felt like her old self.

She shook her head, trying to dislodge those thoughts. There was a reason she'd walked away from ghost hunting and Cash. The former was too dangerous, and the latter was far too tempting. Both would invite trouble.

Trouble she didn't need.

She'd made a promise to her sister, and she intended to keep it. That was why she'd remained closed off for the past three months every time he'd walked into Equinox. She hadn't done more than ask what he wanted to drink and hand him a check. Well, that and refuse to be his ghost-hunting partner again.

Her phone started to ring through the speakers of the car, playing *Grounded* by Silver Scars, the band that Levi Kelley had formed with a friend of his.

I knew it was time to leave it all behind
The leaves are fallin'
I can't shake your words from my mind
And now you're callin'
Telling me I take too many risks
That all you need is for me to be grounded

HARLOW DIDN'T NEED to look at the screen to know who was calling. She hit the Accept button on her steering wheel and said, "Hey, sis. Happy solstice."

"You know I don't celebrate," Imogen said.

"Okay." Harlow kept her tone light, knowing that if she showed any hint of irritation at her sister that she'd hang up and it would be months before she heard from her again. "What's up? Anything exciting?"

"Not exciting, no," Imogen said, sounding glum.

"What's wrong?" Harlow asked. There was something about her sister's resigned tone that had dread building up in her gut.

"Did you ever find a bigger place than that studio you're renting?" Imogen asked hesitantly.

"Yes! As a matter of fact, I did. Just got the keys today. Two bedroom, two bath place that's out on the edge of the redwoods. I heard there's a waterfall not too far from the back property line, so I imagine I'll spend a lot of time exploring once I'm settled in."

Imogen snorted. "Once you're settled in? I bet you're out there tonight looking for that waterfall."

It *was* the equinox, and there was no better way to do an overall cleanse than to do it outside under the moon. But Harlow didn't take the bait. Her sister wanted nothing to do with ghosts or magic after what had happened the year before. She certainly didn't want to hear about Harlow performing an annual cleanse. She cleared her throat. "Enough about me. I want to hear about you. What's got you sounding so deflated?"

"I hate that you know me so well," Imogen said, sounding a little annoyed.

Harlow chuckled softly. "I'm sorry. Should I not have asked?"

"No, that's not... Ugh. I lost my job."

"What? Why?" Harlow pulled into the long driveway of her garage apartment rental and cut the engine of her Subaru.

"It's nothing I did," Imogen rushed out. "The family is selling out to a big winery, and they already have staff to handle the weddings, so I've been downsized, I guess." There was a tremble in her voice, and Harlow knew she was barely keeping it together.

"I'm so sorry, sis. Is there anything I can do?"

"Like what? Ask a ghost to see if there are any openings?" she asked sarcastically. "No thanks."

Harlow ground her teeth together. Her sister had been itching for a fight for months. So far, Harlow had managed to head her off every time, but after dealing with two rogue ghosts and letting her guard down for Cash, she just didn't have it in her to take the high road this time. "That's not fair, Imogen, and you know it. I gave all that up over a year ago."

"That's temporary, and we *both* know it," Imogen snapped.

Anger coiled in Harlow's gut and seemed to crawl up her throat until her face heated. "I don't know what you want from me, Imogen. I gave up my entire life last year for you, including Cash." Her voice broke, and she silently cursed herself for showing her sister any emotion when it came to Cash Moses.

"I never asked you to do that, Harlow," Imogen said fiercely. "So don't blame me for your failed relationship."

Her sister's words stabbed her right in the chest because it was true. Imogen hadn't wanted her to leave Cash, but she'd had to. When she'd promised her sister she'd leave ghost hunting behind, there hadn't been any choice. If she'd stayed with Cash, she'd be right back where she was before. Right back where she was just an hour earlier. She and Cash had spent so many years fighting ghosts that it just seemed to be something they couldn't walk away from even if they wanted to. Not when they were together. So even though Imogen hadn't explicitly asked her to leave Cash, she had indirectly, because there was no relationship with Cash without ghosts haunting them. She'd never say it, but the truth was Harlow had given it all up for Imogen. But despite that, her only living relative and the person she loved most in the world still resented her. Harlow steeled herself and said, "I don't blame you. I've made my own choices, and that's on me. Listen, I'm sorry you lost your job. When's your last day?"

There was a long pause, and then Imogen said, "Six weeks ago."

Harlow leaned back in the seat, taking in the information. Her sister had been out of work for weeks and had just now decided to tell her? "I see."

"Don't be like that," Imogen demanded, getting some of her

fire back. "I didn't tell you because I was hoping to have a new job lined up before I gave you the news. You know, so you didn't go all big sister on me and try to fix everything."

Harlow closed her eyes and just felt exhausted. It had been a year of this same conversation. The details changed, but the subtext was always there. In Imogen's eyes, Harlow was the overbearing, meddling sister who didn't trust Imogen to keep herself out of trouble. The worst part was that there was more than a grain of truth to that assessment, and no amount of Harlow trying to prove to her sister that she'd changed had worked. Imogen didn't trust her. Not fully. And Harlow couldn't blame her. Not after the way things went down last year. "I'm sorry," she said quietly. "I guess by your tone that you haven't been successful in finding anything."

"No."

Harlow waited for her to continue, knowing that Imogen wouldn't be telling her now if she'd had any other choice. "What can I do?"

"Nothing," Imogen said automatically and then cursed softly under her breath. "I mean, there's not really anything you can do to fix this, but since I haven't found anything, and trust me, I've been looking, I'm not going to be able to afford to stay here. I was wondering if…"

Her sister's voice trailed off, and the silence between them was deafening. Harlow refused to finish that sentence for her sister. She had no trouble believing that Imogen had gone all out looking for a new job. Her sister wasn't one to ask for help. If she was asking now, it meant things were getting dire.

"Ugh! Did you say that house you've rented has a second bedroom?" Imogen finally asked.

"It does. And you know my door is always open to you," Harlow said, both elated that her sister had come to her for help and also anxious about the idea of Imogen living with her. If she continued to fling verbal jabs at Harlow, it was going to make for a very uncomfortable living situation. But in no world would she ever refuse to help her sister, so she put on a smile and asked, "When can I expect you?"

Imogen let out a long sigh. "Tomorrow. I've already packed."

"I'll text you the address."

"Thanks," Imogen said, and the line went dead.

It wasn't going to be the reunion that Harlow dreamed of, but hopefully, it would be a step in the right direction to repair their relationship.

Harlow climbed out of the vehicle, hurried up the stairs, and swept into the small apartment, ready to pack an overnight bag. But the moment she stepped into the room, all hell broke loose.

A small lamp flew across the room, barely missing her as it smashed against the wall, the ceramic base shattering into small pieces. The overhead lights flickered on and off, followed by her cabinet doors opening and her cheap box-store dishes falling out to the tile floor.

"Enjoy it while you can!" Harlow yelled as fury raced through her when she instantly recognized the rancid energy in the room. She'd last felt it just over a year ago, right after she'd expelled the spirit from her sister's body. "Just because I can't see you or talk to you, it doesn't mean I can't make your existence hell!"

The threat was likely toothless, but that didn't mean Harlow wouldn't try. Despite the protections she'd used to keep her apartment spirit free, it was clear that the thinning veil of the equinox had given this particular spirit far too much energy. The sage she burned nearly every day hadn't helped and neither had the protection circle.

The couch pillows flew directly at Harlow, hitting her square in the face. *At least they were just pillows,* she told herself as she tried to dodge them.

"What else have you got?" Harlow taunted, hoping that the more energy the spirit used, the sooner she'd flame out and disappear until the next time she gathered enough energy to attack Harlow.

The gas stove turned on with a *whoosh* of flame, and then just as suddenly, the flame went out. Harlow hurried to the stove and turned the knob, shutting down the gas so that the spirit didn't end up blowing up the apartment. Just as she turned back around, a knife whizzed past her head and lodged into the cabinet to her right.

"Oh, that's quite enough," Harlow called, instinctively reaching for her spike in her torn pocket. But as soon as she wrapped her fingers around the cool handle, she let it go again, knowing it would be of no use. This particular spirit seemed to be immune to her iron spike. Even though Harlow couldn't see her, she could feel the spirit's presence, and the last time they'd met, Harlow had staked her to the wall only to find out her magic didn't work on this one. In fact, Harlow had barely escaped the encounter without being possessed herself, and the magic she had used to try and fend off the spirit had left her far too weak for days afterward.

Fighting this ghost had made her more than a little vulnerable. Her two main tools, her spike and the magic she used to banish ghosts, were completely useless. Instead, she reached for the salt and a sage stick she'd left on the counter, praying they would help at least slow her down.

As Harlow's hand tightened around the salt, the container

was nearly yanked out of her grasp by the spirit. Harlow tightened her hold and then flung a substantial amount of salt in the spirit's direction.

The effect was immediate. The energy ball took a significant hit, and the lights stopped flickering.

Harlow advanced, making a salt circle around the energy ball. It still pulsed with activity, but the shenanigans ceased altogether.

"That's it? Salt is your downfall?" she called out, but she knew in her gut that wasn't quite right. Hadn't she used a salt circle the last time she'd battled the spirit? The only thing that had expelled the spirit was using her own magic to shield herself and then waiting until the spirit ran out of energy and faded back into the shadow world. The fact that Harlow could contain her in a circle this time was a new development. But why? What was the difference this time?

She didn't know and didn't really want to wait to find out.

Harlow hurried over to the dresser and hastily shoved enough clothes to last a few days into a bag. Then, after checking on the spirit to make sure she was still contained, she ran into the bathroom to collect her toiletries. The last thing she grabbed on her way out was a cigar box she kept in a drawer in the kitchen.

With one last look back at the spirit, Harlow closed the door on the mess and ran back to her Subaru. Once she was strapped in and racing down the road, she noticed her shaking hands.

She let out a long, slow breath and had an intense urge to call Cash. He'd been right; she shouldn't have spent the night alone. Not when the veil to the afterlife was so thin. One phone call was all it would take, and he'd be there. She knew that without a doubt. Still, she dismissed the thought. Now that the spirit was contained, at least for the moment, it wasn't likely she'd have the strength to find Harlow at her new place that night. By then the veil would have strengthened, and it was likely the spirit would have a much harder time getting through her defenses. Especially if she laid a thick salt circle around her new home.

Satisfied with her decision, Harlow forced herself to loosen her grip on the steering wheel as she rolled her shoulders, trying to let go of some of the tension.

This was not the way she'd planned to celebrate the equinox.

CHAPTER 4

*T*wenty minutes later, Harlow stood in front of her new home with a bag of salt in her hands. It had been in her cargo area and was a holdover from her ghost-hunting days. After everything she'd witnessed over the life of her ghost-hunting career, there were just some things she couldn't live without. A large bag of salt in the back of her vehicle was one of them. The others were a well-stocked supply of sage and plenty of white pillar candles. Those three things were the basics when faced with an unwelcome spirit.

After laying a thick layer of salt around the house, she left a small opening right at the front door. Then she got to work on smudging the place. It took four bundles of sage to cleanse the house to her satisfaction, and when she was done, she lit one of the candles and chanted, *"Eicere, eicere, eicere."* The words echoed around the room, preemptively banishing any spirit that might have been hanging around the home.

Though she had her doubts that any had moved in. The place was relatively new. It had only been built ten years prior, and the owners had lived in it for five years before moving and turning it into a rental. As far as she knew, nothing unusual had happened in that time and no one had died. The likelihood of it being haunted was low. It was one of the reasons she'd desperately wanted to rent it.

Once she was satisfied the home was cleansed, she walked back outside and closed the small section of the salt circle.

Exhausted, she sat on the steps that led up to the house and looked up to see an almost full moon. The bright light was enough to shake some of her weariness, and she had the sudden desire to find that waterfall.

Imogen had been correct.

The very idea of Harlow resisting celebrating the equinox with a good physical cleanse under the moonlight was laughable. Even though she'd hung up her ghost-hunting career, she was still a witch, wasn't she? Harlow went inside, grabbed a tote, and filled it with her supplies. Once she was on the well-marked trail and could hear the soothing sounds of the waterfall, the remaining tension started to ease from her limbs.

There was just something about walking under the moonlight that always seemed to put her at ease. And even though she knew she should be wary of encountering more spirits on such a night, the magic that was woven into the very fiber of Keating Hollow was intoxicating enough that she couldn't bring herself to worry further. Besides, the one spirit she didn't want to encounter was trapped in her old apartment and wouldn't be coming for her tonight. She was confident she could handle anything else.

When the path opened up to a small clearing and Harlow spotted the moonlight shimmering off the waterfall, happy tears stung her eyes. She had never felt like she'd just belonged somewhere like she did in this enchanted town. At this place, where the redwoods soothed her soul and the river fed her magic.

When she'd left the small town of Ojai, California, six months ago, she hadn't been at all sure where she was going to end up. She'd spent some time driving up the coast of California, trying to decide what might be a good fit. There was a place on the central coast called Premonition Pointe that she'd thought had potential. In fact, it had been a strong possibility. She'd first thought that after she spent some more time exploring she'd end up back there. But then she'd found her way to Keating Hollow as if it had been a beacon, and she'd never left.

Considering Harlow and Imogen's childhood had been spent moving around every few years, they didn't really have a place they called home. If pressed, Harlow would have said her grandmother's house in Ojai, but even that old Craftsman that her grandmother had loved hadn't ever really felt right. It had too many ghosts that passed through, always demanding Harlow's attention. While her grandmother had made her feel loved and safe, the home itself had never been comfortable for Harlow.

It was strange how Harlow could move to Keating Hollow, a place where she'd known no one, and instantly fit in. Sure, she'd heard of Silas Ansell, Levi Kelley, Cameron Copeland, and Miranda Moon, but that was just because they worked as screenwriters or actors in the same entertainment industry that she had. But she hadn't ever met them and hadn't expected to. Celebrity ghost hunters didn't exactly run in the same circles as movie stars and rock stars. Or at least they didn't usually. But she'd met all of them now that she managed the pub.

Harlow had just moved past the trees when a large white

wolf appeared near the waterfall with his ears laid back as he stared Harlow down. She stopped in her tracks, watching and waiting. The wolf wasn't snarling, but he was on alert.

Her heart started to race. What was one supposed to do when they encountered a wolf? Stand still and wait or slowly back away? She was still trying to decide, but then the wolf relaxed and his ears returned to normal.

Movement to the left caught her attention, and Harlow's panic started to make her palms sweat. If the wolf had pack members, this night had just taken a turn for the worst. But when she glanced over, there weren't any other wolves, only a barefoot woman with long, dark, and very wet hair who was wearing a dark green robe. Droplets clung to her exposed skin, making it obvious she'd just stepped out of the water.

"He's not dangerous," the woman said, placing a hand on the wolf's head and stroking one of his ears. The wolf leaned into her, pressing his body against her leg.

Harlow blinked at the woman and then the wolf. She'd never met a domesticated one. "I'm sorry. Is this your property? I didn't mean to trespass."

"Oh no. It's public land." The woman moved closer and stretched her hand out. "I'm Zya Rossi. You're Harlow, right? The one that runs that new pub, Equinox?"

"Yes." Harlow shook her hand. "Nice to meet you, Zya. You own the yarn shop, right?" Harlow hadn't spent any time at Witches in Stitches, but the name Zya was unusual enough that she'd recognized it from her patrons' conversations.

"I do." She smiled and placed her hand on the wolf's head again. "This is Silver by the way."

Harlow looked at the wolf's intelligent eyes and wondered how the woman had ended up with a wolf. "Hello, Silver."

The wolf relaxed his stance as his tongue lolled out of his

mouth, looking more like a playful puppy than a dangerous wolf.

"I didn't mean to interrupt anything," Harlow said. "I can come back when you're done here."

"You didn't interrupt. I just finished my solstice ritual," Zya said. "Silver was keeping an eye out for me." She smiled down at the wolf and then eyed Harlow's tote bag. "Not that we expected anyone to be here. I assume that's why you're here, too. The waterfall *is* the perfect place for it."

Harlow normally wouldn't confide in a woman she'd just met, but for some reason, she felt instantly comfortable around Zya. It happened sometimes. As though maybe her soul recognized a like-soul. "Yes, actually. I was going to do a cleanse so that I can head into spring with less baggage, so to speak."

The other woman chuckled. "Well, let us get out of your way, then. Unless you want me and Silver to stand guard over the clearing?"

"Oh no," Harlow said, waving a hand. "I really don't think there's any reason for that, do you? Not in Keating Hollow anyway. For a magical town, this place is surprisingly tame."

Zya let out a bark of laughter but then quickly sobered. "I suppose that's true enough. Though I will say that it's not unheard of for things to go haywire here. And when they do, because of the magical element, they can be hard to spot. You know that saying, 'things aren't what they seem?'"

"Yeah."

"You can think everything is fine, and then you find out that your future mother-in-law has cursed you to be possessed by a crazy spirit so she can use your actions against you and her son in a custody lawsuit for her grandchild."

Harlow blinked at her. "Please tell me that didn't happen."

"Oh, it did," she said with a humorless laugh. "It didn't work, thank the goddess, but it did make me a little more cautious when it comes to dealing with angry family members."

"That's something I can relate to," Harlow said, suppressing a wince. It had been a year since Imogen had been possessed, causing her to become a completely different person, and Harlow was still ashamed of how she'd handled the situation. "I suppose you're right. Even a peaceful and enchanting place like Keating Hollow must have its share of problems."

"Magic always kicks things up a notch." Zya pointed to a spot just off the path that was protected by trees and said, "How about Silver and I just wait over there? It will give you privacy, but we'll be able to warn you if we see anyone or anything unusual."

Harlow's instinct was to decline the offer, but instead, she found herself nodding. "Thank you."

"No problem at all. Come on, Silver." The pair of them disappeared into the trees. They were silent and had an almost ethereal quality about them. She had no doubt they were excellent at hiding in plain sight. If they didn't want to be seen, they wouldn't be.

Feeling just a little more connected to her community, Harlow moved toward the waterfall and started to unpack her supplies.

CHAPTER 5

*C*ash pulled into the driveway of the old two-story farmhouse that had been in his family for nearly a century and killed the engine of his Jeep. It was still surreal to him that he'd ended up in Keating Hollow. When Harlow left him a year ago after they'd lost their paranormal ghost hunters show, he'd been devastated by her complete abandonment of their lives together. It hadn't taken long for that devastation to turn to anger, and he'd been convinced that they were one hundred percent over. How could he ever trust anyone who'd just walked out like she had?

Not that she'd shown any interest in reconciling. In fact, she hadn't contacted him at all. She'd walked away cold turkey and that, more than anything, had fueled his anger.

But then fate had stepped in when he and his brother inherited a great-aunt's home. One that just happened to be in Keating Hollow. It wasn't until he'd come to check on the condition of the house so they could decide if they wanted to keep it or sell it when he realized Harlow had settled there just a few months earlier.

He'd known it was a sign.

And Cash Moses didn't ignore signs. Their paths were destined to cross again. He knew that plain as day the moment he ran into her and discovered she was working at Equinox. That's when he knew he hadn't been angry. Not really. He'd been hurt.

But so had she.

He saw that now. She'd asked him to give up ghost hunting, to leave it all behind, and he'd refused. He'd been adamant that they could pick up and start over. That all she needed was a little time. That she'd come back to him when she had time to think it through.

She hadn't. Instead, she'd started over in Keating Hollow.

And now, so had he. Somehow or another, he'd find a way to heal them both from the devastation of the year before. He just needed to figure out how to gain her trust again.

Cash put all of his ponderings aside and hopped out of the Jeep, still wishing that Harlow would've let him stay with her for the evening. After the scene at the pub, he was more than a little worried about how the rest of her night would go. He knew she could handle herself if more ghosts showed up, but he hated the idea of her having to fight them alone.

Rubbing a hand over his stubbled jaw, he made his way into the farmhouse, clicking on the entry light when he was inside. The place was silent, but he immediately knew he wasn't alone.

Spinning, he reached into his pocket for the iron chain and came up empty, belatedly remembering that it had been destroyed back at the pub.

"Whoa, big brother," Shaun said, holding his hands up in the air. "There are no ghosts here."

"Shaun? What the hell, man?" he barked out, his body

trembling slightly from the rush of adrenaline. "You couldn't have tried calling instead of startling me like that?"

"I'm sorry. I didn't realize I needed to make an appointment to use my own house." Shaun's tone was flat as he narrowed his eyes at his brother.

Cash rolled his eyes. "That's not what I meant, and you know it." He crossed into the kitchen and went straight for the coffee maker. He'd missed his afternoon dose of caffeine and if he didn't get his fix, he'd be nursing a massive headache in the morning. As he measured the coffee grounds, he glanced at his brother. "Why were you just sitting in the dark?"

Shaun shrugged one shoulder. "I didn't intend to. I suppose the night just snuck up on me."

"Is your truck in the garage?" Cash didn't for one minute believe that his brother just forgot to turn on a light. He hadn't called to let Cash know he was coming, his truck was MIA, and he'd sat in the chair in the corner of the living room with no lights on, apparently just waiting for Cash to get home. None of that had been an accident.

"Yes. Is that a problem?"

Cash raised one eyebrow. "That's interesting. Where'd you put the furniture?"

"What furniture?" Shaun asked slowly.

"Aunt Jane's furniture. I put it in the garage before all of this was delivered." Cash waved a hand at the living room. The first thing he'd done was clear out all of Aunt Jane's 1970s furniture and replaced it with a new overstuffed couch and matching chairs.

Shaun muttered a curse under his breath. "Fine. You caught me. I didn't park in the garage. I couldn't even get in it because you have that padlock on it, and I don't have the key. Why? I have no idea, but maybe it's because my brother didn't think to leave one for me."

Cash ignored his outburst and asked, "So where is it?"

"Behind the garage. I figured you'd never see it there."

"I wouldn't say never," Cash said. "But the real question is, why? Because if this was supposed to be a surprise, I'd say your tactics need a little work."

"You *were* surprised, though, right?" Shaun walked over and poured his own cup of coffee.

Cash grabbed the cheese pastry he had sitting on the counter, and both of them took a seat at the kitchen table. He pushed the pastry tin toward Shaun and said, "Spill it. What's going on?"

Shaun closed his eyes, took a sip of his coffee, and said, "I thought I had a premonition, but it turns out I was wrong."

Cash sat up straight, giving his brother his full attention. Shaun didn't have premonitions often, but when he did, they were usually spot on. "What did you see?"

"It doesn't matter. It wasn't real. I knew it the moment I walked into the house, but I still needed to be sure. That's why I was sitting in the dark, waiting to make sure nothing happened. When you walked in and no ghost appeared, I knew for sure."

"I don't understand," Cash said, frowning at his brother. "You came here because you had a premonition that a ghost was going to attack me?"

"Yes," he said simply and took a bite of cheese danish.

Cash grinned at his brother. "So you really do care." He pressed a hand to his heart and pretended to swoon.

"You are my only brother. I guess it would be nice to keep you around," Shaun said.

"Tell me about the premonition. What did you see?" Cash

asked, unable to help himself. He knew Shaun didn't like talking about them if he could help it, but Cash had to know what he'd seen.

"This one was really weird. So weird that I'm not sure I didn't just doze off a bit and dream the entire thing."

Cash was silent, waiting for the rest of the story.

It took a few seconds, but Shaun did finally elaborate. "This one was so weird because I saw it from what I *thought* was your perspective, almost as if I was seeing the scene through your eyes."

"That's unusual," Cash agreed. Usually he just saw his premonitions like a mini movie. This sounded like he was *in* the premonition instead of just seeing it.

"Yeah. Anyway, you came into a dark house, headed to the kitchen, and reached for the coffee pot. The moment you touched it, things just started flying all around. Nothing you did could stop it, and within moments I felt you get clobbered over the head with something heavy. Then everything went dark."

"You mean I was knocked out?" Cash glanced around the room, his eyes landing on the old kettle he'd kept because he liked having something of Aunt Jane's in the kitchen, even if he'd never use it. Was that what had taken him out in Shaun's vision? Maybe.

"Yeah. But like I said, I knew it wasn't true the moment I walked in here because the place looks nothing like what I saw in the premonition. The kitchen was much more modern and had all stainless steel appliances. This"—he waved a hand at the cabinetry—"is much more traditional. Classy, but traditional."

This was Shaun's first visit to Aunt Jane's house since he was about five years old. The fact that he hadn't remembered what the kitchen looked like wasn't a surprise. Cash had sent him a file of pictures, but knowing his brother, he hadn't taken any time to look at them. Prior to showing up in Keating Hollow, he hadn't shown much interest in the old house.

"Okay, that settles it then. I'm voting it was a dream," Cash said, knowing that Shaun's premonitions always came true within a few hours. "But I'm not going to complain that it got you here. Let me take you on a tour of the house."

Shaun followed him around the house, not saying much until they paused at the room that Cash had fixed up for him. One wall was painted stormy gray, Shaun's favorite color, while the rest was white. He'd put in a queen-size bed with a new mattress and added an armchair by the window. It looked nice if Cash did say so himself.

"You've done a great job fixing this place up," Shaun said finally. "Mind if I stay a while?"

"It's your house, too. No need to ask me," Cash said automatically as he suppressed a smile. Having his brother there with him wasn't what he'd expected, but he definitely wasn't complaining about it. It had been years since they'd spent any significant time together. Maybe this was just what they needed to reconnect after years of them both working too hard.

Shaun shook his head at him. "I know it's my house, too, but you're the one living here full time. Also the one who's taken over fixing it up. I didn't want to just barge in on you, especially if you've patched things up with Harlow."

Cash pressed his lips together in a thin line and shook his head. "We haven't patched anything up. But we're at least on speaking terms."

"You haven't?" Shaun's brow furrowed. "That doesn't..." He shook his head again and let out a barely audible groan. "I swear, my seer ability is in the toilet. I thought for sure I saw a vision of her kissing you. Not the sweet innocent kind either. This one was just this side of an R rating."

"Maybe it'll still happen," Cash said, unable to keep the hope from rising in his chest.

"Maybe, but it won't be tonight—" Shaun suddenly stopped talking, and his eyes became unfocused as he gripped the doorframe.

"Dammit!" Cash immediately wrapped his arm around his brother's waist when he recognized the signs of an intense premonition. Shaun's body swayed, and if Cash hadn't been holding on to him, he would have face-planted in two seconds flat.

Cash held Shaun up for what felt like hours but was likely only about thirty seconds. But when someone you care about looked like they've been possessed, thirty seconds felt like an eternity.

Finally, Shaun's eyes fluttered open. He looked over at Cash, blinking to focus, and then said, "It's Harlow. She's in danger."

CHAPTER 6

*C*ash sped down the back roads of Keating Hollow, desperate to get to Harlow. He knew he should have never left her side. Not after what went down at the pub. He tightened his grip on the steering wheel and said a silent prayer of thanks that he had previously taken it upon himself to find out where she lived, despite the fact that it made him feel a little bit like a stalker.

If there was anything he'd learned over his years of ghost hunting, it was that one could never be too prepared. Knowing where she lived just made good sense. That fact was proven when Shaun had his vision and Harlow's phone had gone straight to voice mail.

He hadn't hesitated. The moment Shaun indicated that Harlow was in trouble, Cash had bolted. Shaun hadn't tried to tag along, and Cash hadn't offered. He'd rather his brother stay home, safe from whatever was going down at Harlow's place. Once Cash got there, he'd be putting all his efforts into helping Harlow and didn't need a distraction in the form of his brother, who had never wanted anything to do with ghosts.

The horror of what had happened to Harlow's sister was enough for him to insist that his brother never get involved with any spirit, especially a vindictive one. Since he was a seer and not a ghost hunter, there wasn't much he could do anyway.

The five-mile drive seemed to take hours. Cash stepped on the gas, taking the curves faster than he should. And when his Jeep swerved due to his reckless driving, he just tightened his grip and kept his foot on the gas.

Harlow was in danger. Nothing, not even curvy back roads, were going to slow him down. When he finally reached Harlow's long driveway, he whipped the Jeep in and skidded to a stop. A quick glance told him the Subaru she'd been driving earlier wasn't in sight. The ball of unease that had settled in his gut grew as he bounded out of the vehicle and ran up the stairs to her apartment.

His insistent knocking went unanswered. Cash pulled his phone out, hit her number, and was once again greeted by her voice mail.

"Dammit." Unwilling to just leave without checking to make sure that Harlow wasn't lying hurt inside, he pulled out a set of lock picks and went to work on the door. Over the years, the tools had come in handy more times than he could count. Surely Harlow would understand his need to invade her privacy once she heard about Shaun's premonition. She'd witnessed his gift—or curse—almost as many times as Cash had. She knew just how accurate his visions were.

The lock clicked and Cash burst into the apartment, only to be hit with a wave of nausea. The place was a mess. There were broken dishes strewn all over the kitchen. A few lamps had shattered. And the furniture was askew as if there had been a struggle. Swallowing the bile that had collected at the back of his throat, he rushed into the bedroom, confirming that

Harlow wasn't in the apartment. And judging by the open drawers in her dresser and the random pieces of clothing that had fallen to the floor, he guessed she'd left in a hurry.

Cash stalked back into the living room and narrowed his eyes as he scanned the area, taking note of all the details. The door hadn't shown signs of a forced entry. Most of the items that had been smashed or tossed to the ground were relatively lightweight. And just near the kitchen, he saw it. Evidence of salt thrown all over and a thicker layer of a salt circle, one that had surely been drawn for protection.

He slowly walked over to the area and stopped a foot away from the circle.

The nausea he'd felt when he first entered intensified so much that he nearly stooped over in pain.

"You're back," Cash said.

The wave of nausea intensified again, and he knew he was right. The spirit that had destroyed his life a year ago was trapped in Harlow's kitchen.

"I don't know when or how," he promised the spirit, "but one way or another, I'm going to find a way to banish you for good."

Wind rushed through the open door, the force so strong that it nearly knocked him over. His entire body tensed, ready for a fight. But the wind suddenly vanished, and he wasn't quite sure, but he thought he saw a glimmer of light in the circle, indicating that the spirit was still there.

"Good for Harlow. Looks like she figured out how to trap you at least. That will help when I finally send you to hell where you belong," he said with a low growl before he walked out.

As he climbed back into his Jeep, he let out a sigh of relief that it didn't appear that something terrible had happened to Harlow.

But still, he knew he'd never rest until he was certain that she was okay. And for the first time since she'd walked out of his life, he did something he'd told himself he wouldn't do. He opened his phone, hoping that she hadn't disabled his ability to see her location. To his immense relief, a small dot appeared on his screen, indicating that she was on the far side of town. Or at least her phone was.

Would she be angry if he just showed up at her location?

Yes.

There was no doubt about it. Likely she'd be mad he'd tracked her, but that little bit of technology was a holdover from when they'd been together and hunting ghosts. They'd used it as a safety measure, and it had come in handy many times. Still, he knew she wouldn't appreciate the invasion of privacy, though she could have turned it off at any time. But she hadn't. And neither had he.

It didn't matter if she was angry. Cash just couldn't live with himself until he knew for certain that she was all right.

After setting his GPS to her location, he put the Jeep in gear and took off across town.

When he pulled into the long drive of the cute house that sat at the base of the forest, he was gratified to see Harlow's Subaru parked out front. But when he went to the door and no one answered his knock, that unease began to settle in his gut again.

Now what?

Peeking in the windows only told him what he'd already known. Harlow wasn't there. No one was. The only thing he saw was her overnight bag. The one he'd given her at Christmas two years ago. He'd bought it to replace the ratty one that was so old the wheels had broken and the threads were starting to fray. At least he knew she had somewhere safe to stay other than her tiny apartment that was now housing a trapped spirit.

He pulled his phone out again and confirmed that her phone was indeed inside the house. Had she gone somewhere with whoever she was staying with?

Or had someone forced her to go somewhere?

His tracking skills kicked in and he looked around the dirt road, checking for fresh tire tracks. The only ones he saw were from his own vehicle and Harlow's.

Did that mean she wasn't staying with someone else? Maybe she was renting the house for the night.

Convinced there wasn't any foul play by the lack of any sort of struggle, he walked around the house to check for any other clues.

He turned on the flashlight app on his phone and scanned the area. Just outside the back door, he spotted the single set of footprints that led right into the forest.

Cash let out a sigh of relief as the tension started to drain from his taut muscles.

The forest made sense. It was the solstice after all.

He was willing to bet his shirt that if he followed the narrow trail that eventually he'd find water and Harlow.

He hesitated for just a moment, knowing that if Harlow was doing a ritual, she would not want to be interrupted. But he just couldn't turn around and go home until he proved to himself that she wasn't in danger.

Squaring his shoulders, he moved quickly down the moonlit trail.

He heard the waterfall before he spotted it. The rush of the water filled the silent forest, and he knew without a doubt that Harlow was just beyond the trees. He could sometimes just sense when she was around. His soul soothed and he just felt *right.*

Cash knew he could have turned around then. Harlow was just beyond the trees, clearly not in any danger. He'd have felt that, too. But he was too close now. The odds were good that she'd already felt his energy, and if he retreated now, it would leave too many lingering questions between them. He didn't want her to think he was spying on her.

The trees opened up to a small moonlit lagoon with a waterfall on the far side. His eyes immediately focused on Harlow and her bare skin under the spray of the waterfall. Her eyes were closed, and her hands were raised high in the air as she chanted a cleansing spell in Latin.

Her eyes opened, and Harlow stared straight at him. Her lips turned down into a frown as she lowered her arms and crossed them over her bare chest.

Cash couldn't help it when his gaze scanned her body, the one he hadn't touched in over a year. Unconsciously he took a step forward, his entire being drawn to her with an intense magnetic pull. But before he could move more than a few inches, a flash of white came from the woods to his left, followed by a snarling growl.

His eyes focused on the large white wolf that stood in front of him with its hackles raised and its teeth bared.

"Whoa," Cash said, holding his hands up as he took a small step backward. "I mean no harm."

The wolf snarled again and inched closer.

Cash stood his ground, knowing that if he showed any weakness the wolf would likely lunge for him.

"Who are you and why are you here?" a female voice of steel asked just before a woman appeared from the trees. She had long black hair and her green eyes pierced him with suspicion.

"Cash Moses," he said automatically. "I'm a... friend of Harlow's." He nodded his head toward the waterfall.

"Friend?" She raised one eyebrow as the wolf started to growl again. "Something tells me that *friend* isn't the word Harlow would use."

"It's not," Harlow said from behind them. She was wrapped in a green robe and was scowling at him. "He's my ex, and for the life of me, I can't understand why he's here or how he even found me."

"Harlow, I can explain," Cash started.

"You know what, Cash? I'm not sure I even care. Please just go," she said with a tired sigh. "You've already interrupted my ritual. Don't make things worse by trying to justify this gross invasion of privacy."

Disappointment mixed with frustration as he stared at her, trying to see past her anger to the person he used to know. The one who'd been so connected to him that she sometimes knew what he was thinking before he even had a chance to process his own thoughts.

"It's like that, is it?" he asked in a flat tone.

"It is." Her jaw was tense, and her eyes flashed with irritation.

"Fine," he said and looked at the wolf. "You can call off your guard dog. I'm going."

He glanced at Harlow one last time. "Shaun had a vision that you were in danger. I'm glad to see that you're okay."

Then he turned on his heel and silently fumed as he strode back to his Jeep, trying to keep from pressing his fingers to the ache that pulsed just below his breastbone.

CHAPTER 7

*H*arlow woke the next morning with a pounding headache and a hollow pit in her stomach. After her run-in with Cash, she'd just felt defeated. As if she'd done something terribly wrong and there was no way to make it right.

She knew she was being hard on herself. Anyone would be upset to find their ex intruding on their ritual cleansing, but when Cash had said that Shaun had a vision she was in danger, Harlow knew Cash had done the only thing he could. He'd tracked her down to make sure she was okay.

Of course he had.

It was who Cash was. He'd have tried to track down anyone who'd been in one of Shaun's visions because they both knew that Shaun was the real deal. No doubt he'd witnessed the scene back at her apartment. Harlow knew that Cash would have gone there first and then tracked her to her new place. Likely with the help of technology.

Harlow sat up in bed, grabbed her phone, and opened the Find My app. There he was. Cash Moses showed up as a dot somewhere across town. He hadn't turned that feature off. Just like she hadn't.

She'd thought about it. More than once. But for some reason, she just couldn't make that change in her settings. Was it that she'd wanted him to find her? Or was it just that after all the changes she'd made to her life, that was just one step too far?

Harlow knew the answer. She hadn't turned it off because it felt like the final nail in the coffin of the most important relationship she'd ever had. Likely the most important one she'd ever have. Severing that final link felt like a death she just couldn't face.

She shut the phone down without making any changes, rolled out of bed, and shuffled into the kitchen, grateful that the house had come furnished with the basics, including a coffee maker. After fixing herself a cup, she shuffled back to the bathroom and hoped the shower combined with the caffeine would help her feel human again.

Forty-five minutes later, Harlow was dressed but only slightly more functional. There was no doubt that fighting off a couple of spirits and then skipping dinner had taken its toll. She'd have to get some food in her soon, or the headache would only get worse.

While the solstice hadn't turned out the way she'd hoped, there was one thing she was grateful for; no spirits had bothered her at her new home. Once she'd come back from her interrupted cleanse, she'd gotten ready for bed and then climbed into the cool sheets. She'd lain there for more than two hours, listening and waiting.

But nothing had shown, and eventually she'd drifted into a fitful sleep. She'd stayed up far too late, hadn't eaten enough, and had worried too much. Now she was paying for it.

Still, there was no time to be sitting around. Her sister was due in town later that day, and she needed to get the house ready. First up were groceries for the fridge. At least enough to last the next couple of days.

Harlow made a list, grabbed her keys, and headed to town. Before making her way to the grocery store, she pulled into an empty parking spot right in front of Incantation Café. If she didn't get something in her stomach, she'd never make it through the aisles without buying out half the store.

The window display featured flower-shaped sugar cookies that were being magically decorated with bright colors of frosting and then arranged into a large bouquet of edible flowers. The magical window displays of Keating Hollow's storefronts never failed to make Harlow smile. Even on days like today when all she wanted to do was hide under the covers and sleep the day away.

The bell chimed as she walked through the door and the scent of spring hit her full force. Someone at Incantation Café was just as ready as she was for the new season. Feeling better already, Harlow made her way to the counter and greeted Hanna Silver, the owner.

"Good morning, Harlow. How are you doing this wonderful spring morning?" the cheerful woman asked. Her dark curly hair was pulled back into a neat ponytail, and her dark eyes glowed with happiness. It was just the sort of infectious energy Harlow needed.

"Better now that I'm here," she said truthfully. "Did you have a good solstice?"

"Absolutely. Rhys and I spent most of it out at the family winery taste-testing the blends we bottled last fall. There are some really good ones this year."

"I can't wait to try them," Harlow said. "Let me know your favorites and I'll order them for Equinox next time."

"You got it." Hanna took her order for an egg and cheese breakfast sandwich along with a chai tea latte. "Have a seat," Hanna said. "I'll bring these out when they're ready."

"Thanks." Harlow paid and was still tucking the change into her wallet when she turned and spotted Cash standing near the front window, two cups of coffee in his hands. Suddenly all of her good cheer seemed to drain right out of her.

"Harlow," he said with a curt nod.

"Cash, I—" Harlow started but was interrupted when Shaun appeared in front of her.

"You had me worried yesterday, angel," Shaun said, pulling her into a hug.

"Sorry about that," she said with a slightly nervous chuckle. "You know how much I hate to worry people."

He pulled back but held her by the shoulders as he stared into her eyes. "I know you've given up on the ghost hunting, but it appears the ghosts haven't given up on you. Is there anything we can do to help?"

Harlow looked past him at Cash, who had taken a seat and was pointedly not looking at them.

"He was out of his mind with worry, you know," Shaun said gently.

"Yeah. I can imagine," Harlow said, her voice so low it was barely a whisper. "I handled it though."

"He said as much." Shaun glanced over his shoulder and then back at her. "Anyway, I'm glad you're okay."

"Thanks." Harlow took a step back just to reclaim a little of her personal space. "It's good to see you." She smiled at Cash's younger brother, who was practically a twin version of her ex. Shaun was just a few inches shorter than Cash and a tad thinner, but he had the same dark eyes and devilish smile. The pair had always been easy on the eyes, and before Harlow had come along, they'd also been the most eligible bachelors in town. "What are you doing in town? Looking for trouble, like the old days?"

He frowned and cut his gaze to his brother for just a moment. "Cash didn't tell you?"

"He told me about the vision, but I didn't know you were here." That unease was back. The one that told her she wasn't going to like what he had to say.

"Oh, uh, well, I'm staying for a bit. You know, to help him fix up that house our aunt left us."

Harlow immediately turned her attention to Cash. "Your aunt left you a house *here* in Keating Hollow? That's why you've been here for the past three months?"

He nodded without even looking at her, and that, more than anything else, infuriated her.

"No way, Cash Moses. Just no way. I don't—how does that even happen? You never told me you had family here," she sputtered before she collected herself. Her tone turned emotionless as she added, "And now you're just staying here... in the town I chose for a fresh start?"

Cash finally lifted his gaze and stared her right in the eye. "Our great-aunt owned a house here and passed about six months ago. She left it to me and Shaun. I know you think that everything I do revolves around you, Harlow, but not this time. I didn't even know you were here when I came to town three months ago to check on the house."

It was on the tip of her tongue to accuse him of staying because of her, but she swallowed her tart reply. Somehow, she just knew he was telling the truth. They never had been very good at lying to each other. But the information was unsettling. Was the universe trying to tell her something? Why else would they have both ended up in the same small town at approximately the same time? "But that night you came into Equinox you told me you were here to search for that ghost. Was that a lie?"

"Yes... and no. I saw you outside of Equinox earlier that day and was shocked as hell. I decided it was a sign that we were supposed to reconnect, seeing as we both ended up in the same town. And to move forward, we'd need to expel that spirit. But you shut me down repeatedly, so I let it go." A small frown claimed Cash's lips before he said, "And I would have told you last night that Shaun was staying for a while, but you didn't exactly give me a chance. Now if you'll excuse us, we have some work to get done on the house."

Shaun glanced between the two of them before stepping in close and giving Harlow a hug and whispering, "It's good to see you."

Tears stung Harlow's eyes, but she blinked them back as she watched the two of them exit the café. Cash, Shaun, and her sister Imogen were her family. Her only family. Or at least they had been until their lives imploded last year. When she moved to Keating Hollow, she'd thought she was on her own. And now, just six months later, they were all coming back to her.

Sort of.

Only now everything was different.

"Harlow?" Hanna said, appearing beside her.

She turned and spotted the gorgeous woman holding her breakfast sandwich and chai tea. Harlow eyed the plate and ceramic mug and instantly regretted not asking for them to go. Gesturing to the table that Cash had just vacated, she took a seat and said, "Thanks."

Hanna placed the items on the table and hesitated for just a moment. "You know what I've learned after living in Keating Hollow for so long?"

Harlow just looked at her, uninterested in any quips of wisdom.

The woman gave her a sympathetic smile and patted her shoulder. "I always hated it when my mother would say things like this, too, but I'm going to say it anyway and you can decide from there."

Harlow let out a tiny sigh and nodded.

"I could lecture you with something cliché like everything happens for a reason, or the day is always darkest before the dawn, but I won't. Instead, I'm just going to say that the best thing about Keating Hollow is that there's always a friend here when you need one. And you, Harlow Thane, look like you could use a night out with the girls. No ghosts. No ex-boyfriends. No anything that's putting that look on your face. Just a night of golf carts, to-go cups, and tarot."

Harlow blinked up at her. "That sounds like trouble."

Hanna gave her a slow grin. "It is. The best kind of trouble. You're off tomorrow night, right?"

"Yes." Equinox was closed on Monday nights, so it wasn't hard to figure out Harlow's schedule.

"Perfect. It's time to let off some steam. Tomorrow night. Meet me and the girls here at eight o'clock."

Harlow opened her mouth to protest. As much as she appreciated the offer, Imogen was coming to town, and she didn't want to ditch her sister.

But Hanna raised her hand and shook her head. "No excuses. If you can make it, just show up. If not, we'll catch you next time." She winked and then retreated back to the counter.

Harlow stared down at her sandwich, grateful for the

invitation but not at all sure how to handle it. Then she glanced up and called, "Hanna?"

"Yeah?"

"Can I bring my sister?"

Hanna's lips curved into a pleased smile. "Absolutely. The more the merrier."

Harlow nodded and let out a slow breath. Maybe it was just the sort of icebreaker she and Imogen needed after their year of tension.

CHAPTER 8

"*W*hat was that about?" Shaun demanded as they headed to the town hardware store.

"What was what about?" Cash asked, feigning ignorance.

His brother let out a huff of irritation. "Listen, I know things have been rough between you and Harlow the past year, but that's no reason to treat her so coldly. It sucks that she broke things off with you, but you could at least try to understand where she's coming from."

Cash ground his teeth together and forced himself not to snap at his brother. Instead, he pulled into a parking space, killed the engine, and turned to Shaun, his tone even when he said, "Listen, Shaun, I know you mean well, but this really isn't any of your business. Harlow and I—we're done. She made that perfectly clear last night."

Shaun narrowed his eyes and shook his head slightly. "You can keep telling yourself that, brother, but anyone with eyes can tell that it's not over. It's never going to be over. Not with that one."

"You don't know what you're talking about," Cash said stubbornly and then climbed out of the Jeep.

Shaun quickly caught up with him and chuckled to himself. "Don't I? We both know that as soon as I have another vision, or if she calls, you'll go running."

Cash paused and closed his eyes for a brief moment. "Please, just let this go."

"I will if you tell me what happened. Last night when you got in, all you said was that Harlow was fine and that she handled the situation."

"You know what happened. Your visions are always accurate," Cash said impatiently, refusing to go into the details of his encounter with Harlow.

Shaun pressed his lips together in a thin line and shook his head. "Not lately. I had two yesterday that haven't manifested. And it's happened a couple of times before when you and Harlow were able to stop a spirit from doing its worst. But the ones yesterday, I don't know. They felt off, and I—"

Cash turned to study his brother, his eyes piercing as suspicion creeped in, and Cash felt a wave of dread wash over him. "Shaun, have you interacted with any spirits lately?"

His brother startled as he took a half step back. "What do you mean? Ghosts are your thing, not mine."

"It's just that…" Cash ran a frustrated hand through his short dark hair. "Dammit. I'm paranoid now."

"Explain."

"You told me last night that one of the visions was from my perspective. And that you saw me and Harlow making out. Those are the two that didn't come true. I'm just wondering if it's at all possible that a spirit was hijacking your visions."

"I don't think so," Shaun said, frowning. "You'd think I'd feel that, wouldn't I?"

"Maybe?" Cash's brow furrowed. "I just don't know. Imogen was possessed last year, and it made her do things wildly out of character. She knew she had a spirit traveling with her, but she couldn't communicate it because the spirit forced her to stay quiet. Harlow and I had never seen anything like it. So I suppose now that your gift is doing unusual things, I'm a bit paranoid."

"I see." Shaun rubbed his stubbled jaw with one hand. "Well, I can honestly say that I don't think I've been possessed. However, I didn't just decide on my own to come to Keating Hollow."

"You didn't?" Cash rubbed his aching breastbone again but didn't even notice until Shaun's gaze landed on his hand.

"You should get that looked at," Shaun said. "If you have a heart attack and die on me, I'm going to be really pissed. Knowing that you'll likely be haunting me is going to put a real crimp in my love life."

Cash let out a huff of surprised laughter. "What love life? You haven't dated anyone since…" He didn't need to finish the sentence. They both knew it'd been over three years since Shaun had caught his fiancée in bed with his best friend. Since then, Shaun hadn't dated anyone. Cash wasn't even sure if he'd had a casual fling.

"I'm not a monk," Shaun confirmed.

"That's good. I was starting to get a little worried about you," Cash said lightly. Then he quickly changed the subject. "Why don't you go back to why you came to Keating Hollow?"

"Grandma told me to," he said with a shrug.

"Grandma Moses?" Cash asked, startled. "When? How?"

"She came to me in a dream. A few nights ago, actually. She said my place was with you in Keating Hollow and that we needed each other. When I woke up, it just felt right. So I told my boss I had a family situation and that I either had to go remote or give notice."

"And she said?" Cash asked, his eyebrows raised. Shaun was a video editor for a production company that mostly worked on commercials and independent films.

"She said we'd give it a try and regroup in ninety days. I hope we have good internet to upload all that video content."

Cash didn't know about that. Internet speeds weren't exactly his specialty. He wasn't worried about it though. He was certain Shaun would figure it out. There were other matters they needed to discuss. "When I asked if you'd interacted with any ghosts recently, you implied you hadn't. Now you're saying Grandma came to you in a dream. So you have. Anyone else?"

Shaun waved an impatient hand. "I thought you meant if I'd *seen* a ghost. Dreaming about Grandma isn't the same thing."

"You don't know that." Cash knew that spirits appeared to people in many different ways. One of them was through dreams. "Are you sure it was her?"

Shaun rolled his eyes. "Stop worrying, brother. I'm not possessed. This isn't an Imogen situation. I promise you. I'm just here because I dreamed that Grandma said I should be here, and it felt right to me. Aren't you always the one saying I need to trust my gut?"

"Yeah. I am." Cash draped his arm around his brother's shoulders and said, "Well, since Grandma sent you here. Might as well put you to work. How do you feel about laying hardwood floors?"

"It sounds like a pain in the ass, but if that's what's on the agenda, then let's get to it."

Cash grinned. And for the first time all week, he felt like maybe, just maybe things were starting to look up for him.

"I'M HEADED DOWNSTAIRS for a drink. Want anything?" Shaun asked.

Cash wiped the sweat from his brow and glanced back at his brother. They'd been ripping up the old damaged floors in the master bedroom and adjacent den for the past two hours. All of it was cleared except for the last part of the den and the walk-in closet, which wasn't big enough for two people. "Sure."

"I'll be back."

Cash heard his brother's footsteps on the stairs as he got to work prying up the last of the boards. Miraculously, most of the subfloor was still in decent shape. There was an area just on the other side of the wall of a hall bathroom that would need to be replaced, but as near as Cash could tell, that was all that needed to be done before they started laying the new boards.

He'd finished the last of the den and was working his way through the walk-in closet when one of the old boards refused to come free. Using the claw end of his hammer, he did his best to pry up a few different areas and then bent down and grabbed the edge with both hands and yanked as hard as he could. The board protested but then ripped out of the floor, sending him backward until he slammed into the wall with a loud *thunk*.

"Son of a..." he muttered, rubbing the back of his head.

Suddenly his skin prickled, and the air turned cold as ice. His vision was still slightly blurred from his contact with the wall, but there was no mistaking the presence in his aunt's house.

A spirit.

The hair stood up on the back of his neck.

But then he heard the very soothing lilt of a vaguely familiar voice. *I always wanted to replace these floors.*

"Aunt Jane?" he asked, squinting to try to focus on the ethereal being floating in front of him. The spirit looked young. Maybe in her midtwenties with long, slightly wavy auburn hair and kind green eyes. Her skin was porcelain, and she looked like she'd just walked right off a movie set.

I know I look a little different, she said with a cheeky grin. *But who wants to look like an arthritic old maid for the rest of eternity?*

"Can't blame you there," Cash said. "If I could be twenty-five again, I might just go for it."

Nah. The best years of your life are still ahead of you. She reached out and pressed an ice cool hand against his cheek.

As weird as it was to feel the presence of a ghost, this one actually comforted him. Aunt Jane felt like family.

I see good things for you.

He opened his eyes and studied her. Did he want to know her predictions?

Her grin widened as her eyes sparkled. *You'll have that family you want, Cash. It might not be traditional, but you'll have everything you need.*

Cash wanted to ask if that family included Harlow, but if she said no, he wasn't sure his heart could take it. Even though he was still angry at the way she'd dismissed him the night before, he knew he'd never stop wanting her.

His brother's footsteps sounded on the stairs again. "Are you finished yet, Cash?" Shaun called out.

I'm really sorry about this, Aunt Jane said with a frown. *But it's for your own good.*

"What—"

An ice-cold wind whipped through the room and the discarded boards started to fly.

Cash stumbled out of the closet and was immediately smacked in the head with one of the boards. He went down hard, too stunned to move.

"Cash! What the hell?" Shaun cried.

In the next moment, through his foggy haze, Cash heard Shaun talking. "Harlow, it's an emergency. Cash has been attacked by a ghost."

Cash tried to push himself up, but a cold weight of energy settled on his chest as his aunt whispered, *It's time to face your past.*

Then his world went dark.

CHAPTER 9

*H*arlow stared once more at the clock. Only five minutes had passed since the last time she'd looked. Her sister was due at the house any minute now, and Harlow just couldn't sit still. She rose from the couch, glanced out the window, and when she didn't see anything other than her Subaru, she retreated to the kitchen, determined to keep her hands busy until she heard the rumble of the 1965 Mustang she missed almost as much as she missed her sister.

Cookies.

That's what she'd do. She'd make cookies. What could be better than walking into a new home that smelled like freshly baked cookies?

Harlow knew cookies weren't going to fix everything that was wrong between her and Imogen, but it was better than waiting at the window like some sort of crazed lunatic.

After finding a mixing bowl and a cookie sheet, Harlow got busy making her sister's favorite. Lemon shortbread. Then, once all the ingredients were already mixed, she started to second guess herself. Would Imogen see this for what it was? Some sort of bribe to get on her sister's good side?

Probably, but it was too late now.

Harlow had just put the cookie sheet in the oven when she heard the loud rumble of the Mustang.

Determined not to look too eager, she started to load the dishwasher. But when she heard the slam of the car door, she couldn't stand it anymore. She wiped her hands on a dishtowel and hurried out the front door. The Mustang was parked next to the Subaru, but her sister was nowhere to be found.

"Imogen?" she called as she rushed down the porch stairs, glancing around.

No answer.

"Hey, sis, where are you?" Harlow moved to stand next to the Mustang and noted that the car was packed with Imogen's personal items. Her purse was still in the front seat, and the car key was still in the ignition.

"Imog—" Harlow started to call again but was cut off by her sister.

"Relax," Imogen said in an irritated tone as she appeared from the side of the house holding a cigarette between two fingers.

Harlow's gaze went right to the cigarette and then she met Imogen's defiant eyes.

"I'm an adult. I'm well aware of the risks involved. I don't need a lecture."

"I wasn't going to say anything," Harlow lied.

"Right. Sure you weren't." Imogen put the cigarette out on the sole of her shoe and then tucked the butt into a baggie she carried in her pocket.

After a silent thankful prayer that Imogen hadn't taken to

smoking in her car, Harlow cleared her throat and said, "Let me help you get this stuff inside."

"You don't have to do that." Imogen went over to the driver's side, grabbed the keys, and then opened the trunk. It was full of suitcases and duffle bags.

"I know I don't have to," Harlow said with a sigh. "I *want* to."

"Suit yourself," Imogen said with a shrug and grabbed a couple of bags before heading inside.

Harlow stared after her, feeling exhausted already. Then she grabbed some bags and followed her sister inside.

Once the car was unloaded and the shortbread cookies were cooling on a rack, Harlow stood in the kitchen, not at all sure what to do with herself. Imogen was holed up in her room, already unpacking. She'd barely said two words to Harlow. And honestly, Harlow was starting to lose patience. She didn't deserve this. Imogen was entitled to her feelings, but she didn't have the right to treat Harlow like a pariah in her own home.

Deciding it was better to catch flies with honey rather than vinegar, she made her sister her favorite cup of tea, put some shortbread cookies on a plate, and then headed for Imogen's room.

"Gen?" Harlow said outside at the door. "I brought you something."

There was no answer.

"Imogen?" Harlow tried again. "I have tea."

She heard movement, but there was still no answer.

"Okay, listen, that's enough of this," Harlow said through the door. "I know you're in there. Ignoring me is beyond childish. Open the door or—"

The door flew open, and Imogen let out a surprised gasp when her eyes met Harlow's. She quickly took the earbuds out of her ears and pressed a hand to her heart. "Damn, Harlow. You startled me."

"I knocked," Harlow said tartly. "Twice."

She held the earbuds up. "I had my music on. Sorry." Then her gaze landed on the plate of cookies and her eyes lit up. "Are those for me?"

"Yes," Harlow said, feeling some of the tension drain from her body as Imogen took one and popped it in her mouth. "I made you blackberry tea, too."

Imogen smiled, something Harlow hadn't seen in months. "Thank you." She grabbed the mug and took a long sip. "You have perfect timing. I was just going to soak in the tub for a bit. My body aches after my drive. Cookies and tea are just what I needed."

Harlow hung back as Imogen took the plate of cookies and disappeared into the bathroom. Then she shook her head and wondered what in the world had just happened. The woman who'd just walked out of her bedroom was not the same one Harlow had met outside just an hour before.

Don't look a gift horse in the mouth, baby. Harlow heard her grandmother's voice in her head and decided her grandmother was right. If Imogen was trying to leave the attitude behind, the best thing Harlow could do was let her.

"What do you want to do for dinner?" Harlow asked her sister when she finally emerged from her bedroom. After taking the world's longest bath, Imogen had once again closed herself up in her room. Harlow assumed she was unpacking but didn't really know.

"Is there some place in town where we can get pizza?" Imogen asked.

"Uh, sure." Harlow thought about all the fresh ingredients she'd purchased earlier that day. "Or I can make tuna salad or tomato basil pasta. I found some freshly made pasta at the grocery store in town—"

"I'm really in the mood for pizza. Come on. I'll even let you drive." Imogen whipped her keys out of her pocket and tossed them to her sister.

Harlow caught them easily and grinned. "You're on."

Both sisters were laughing when Harlow peeled out of the driveway like old times and floored it on the back roads that led to town. "Gods, I missed this," Harlow said with a happy sigh.

Imogen glanced over at her. "You really did, didn't you?"

"Sure. Almost as much as I missed you," she said with a wink, trying to keep it playful.

Imogen groaned. "Don't be cheesy. You know if you want to buy the car back, you can."

"No way. What would you drive?" Harlow shook her head. "Besides, it's not really practical here. I told you that."

Imogen glanced around at the scenery. It was late March, and the well paved roads were clear. "When? For two months of the year? What about the rest of the time? Look at you. I haven't seen you this happy since before…" She trailed off and shook her head. "Never mind. It's just so obvious you love this thing, and I…" She shrugged. "It's okay, but I think I'd like something more modern."

Harlow glanced at her. "Do you have money for something else?"

"Well, no. But eventually. If I can get a job here and save some money, I figured if you bought back the Mustang, I'd at least have a decent down payment. I know my credit's not the greatest right now, not after last year, but if you co-signed... I dunno, it's just a thought."

Was that why Imogen was suddenly being nice to Harlow? She wanted her to help her buy a new car, even though she was living off Harlow and didn't have a job? The thought left a wave of disappointment in the pit of Harlow's stomach, but she didn't ask. Instead, she said, "Yeah, maybe. When you're settled in more, we can talk about it."

Imogen beamed at her.

The truth was Harlow didn't mind helping her sister at all. She'd made a very good living as a celebrity ghost hunter, and during that time, she'd been careful with her money. Her retirement account was funded, and there was more than enough stashed away should Harlow want to buy a house or build something in the future. In practical terms, Harlow didn't have to work. There was enough to fund her simple lifestyle, but the job at Equinox kept her busy and she really enjoyed it. Still, she didn't want to feel taken advantage of, and after a year of getting the cold shoulder from Imogen, the fact that she was suddenly being nice and asking for help just left Harlow feeling cold.

Maybe she was wrong. Maybe this was just Imogen's way of breaking the ice. And it really wasn't her fault that her credit had taken a huge hit. That had been just one of the nasty side effects when the spirit had taken over Imogen's body.

It didn't take long before they were parked and walking into Mystyk Pizza. It was the first time Harlow had visited the town favorite. The walls were covered in stunning burnt-wood art. She was so fascinated she couldn't tear her gaze away.

"Look at the fireplaces," Imogen said. "Whoever spelled those is a powerful fire witch."

Harlow finally looked around and noted that flames in the fireplaces were continuously morphing into familiar scenes from around town. There was even one that depicted a pair of golf carts racing down by the river that made her chuckle.

"Great place, Harlow," Imogen said, touching Harlow's arm.

"It really is, isn't it?"

They followed the hostess to a table near one of the fireplaces and took a seat.

"I wonder if they're hiring," Imogen said as she studied her menu.

Harlow lowered her own menu and peered at her sister. "You're not going to try to find something in the wedding planning industry?"

"In Keating Hollow? I know it's gorgeous here, but it doesn't exactly look like a hotbed of wedding activity."

"You'd be surprised. The Pelshes have a winery. I know they do events there. Other than that, I think most end up having weddings on family property. But I bet they could use a good wedding planner. Maybe you could hang a shingle out and strike out on your own," Harlow suggested.

Imogen snorted. "Sure. And what would I live on until I found some clients?"

"It's just a suggestion," Harlow said, trying to tread carefully. "But if it was something you're interested in, I'm sure we can come up with a business plan. Besides, there's nothing stopping you from getting a part time job while you get it off the ground."

"Hmm, maybe." Imogen went back to studying her menu, and Harlow took that as a good sign.

After they ordered, Imogen leaned forward with her elbows propped on the table. "So if I were to start a wedding planning business, I'd need to scope out places around town that would work for weddings and make a list of possible vendors. Do you know anyone who could help me with that? Someone whose brain I could pick?"

"Sure. Wanda Danvers would be a good one to start with. She's the town realtor and knows everyone. Maybe try Hanna Silver at Incantation Café. Her family owns the winery and she's good friends with the Townsend family. They've been here forever and own The Keating Hollow Brewery."

Imogen nodded as she typed those notes into her phone. "I'd need a website and business cards and some sort of office space." She looked up. "Renting something is out of the question, obviously, but if there's a space we could clear to set up a desk at the house, that would work."

"Sure. There's space in the kitchen," Harlow said, her heart feeling lighter than it had in months. "And as far as a website, I have space on my hosting site. It's paid up for the next three years, so you wouldn't even have to pay for that."

Imogen sobered. "You still have your website?"

Harlow swallowed a groan. "Well, it has a big note that says I've retired, but the site is still there with referrals to other ghost hunters if someone is looking for one. It's a five-year hosting plan that I'd already paid for, so there was no sense in just nuking it all."

"I see." Imogen nodded slowly as if she were processing that information. "That's good, I guess."

"Free is always good," Harlow said flippantly, trying not to get her hackles up. All she was trying to do was help her sister. She didn't know why everything always had to come back to her ghost-hunting past.

"True." Imogen let out a small chuckle. "Well, that's a decent start anyway. I'll need to get in touch with Hanna and Wanda."

"Hey, I was invited to a girls' night with Hanna tomorrow

night. I'm willing to bet Wanda will be there. They said you're welcome. Why don't you come along and talk to them then?"

"Perfect." Imogen put her phone away and smiled up at the waiter who'd just arrived and placed the pizza in front of them. "Looks delicious," she said, eyeing the man with the sun-kissed skin and bright blue eyes instead of the pizza.

Harlow smiled to herself, pleased to see her sister starting to relax.

"If he's any indication of the men in town, I think I'm going to like it here," Imogen said as she watched the waiter retreat. He glanced back at her and winked, causing Imogen's face to turn bright pink.

A laugh bubbled out of Harlow's lips and suddenly both she and Imogen were giggling in a way they hadn't since they were teenagers.

Harlow was still chuckling when her phone started to ring. When's Shaun's name popped up on the screen, she frowned. "Shaun? What's wrong?"

A moment later, she ended the call. "We have to go. Cash is in trouble."

"Cash is here? In Keating Hollow?" Imogen asked, her eyes wide as she rose from her seat.

"Yeah. It's kind of a long story," Harlow said, digging in her bag for her wallet.

What happened?" Imogen asked.

"A ghost attacked him." Harlow threw some money on the table and started to stride toward the door. When she realized Imogen wasn't with her, she glanced back and spotted her sister standing frozen by the table. "Gen?"

"I can't do this again," she said as her face drained of color. "You know how I feel about you hunting ghosts."

"I have to," Harlow said, hating that she'd put her sister in this position. But what else could she do? In a very quiet voice, she added, "It's Cash. If anything happens to him..." She squeezed her eyes shut, trying to ignore the flash of pain that was seizing her heart. Every second that she stood there arguing with Imogen was one more that she was away from Cash when he needed her.

When Harlow opened her eyes, she saw a look of pure terror on Imogen's face. But when her sister spoke, she said, "Fine. For Cash. But then I'll have no choice but to find somewhere else to live. I can't do this again."

Harlow's heart nearly broke in two. She felt like her sister was forcing her to make the choice between her and Cash all over again. But this time, Cash was in danger and there was just no way that Harlow could walk away when she knew she could help. "I'm sorry to hear that, Gen. I really am. I'd promise you it will never happen again, but we both know I can't do that."

Imogen gave her a nod, and without another word she brushed past Harlow and headed outside to the Mustang. Harlow was right on her heels, and after tracking Cash on her phone, she put the car in gear and sped across town.

CHAPTER 10

"What happened?" Cash asked as he pushed himself up into a sitting position. The room swam, and he had to shut his eyes to ward off the dizziness.

"Here, drink this," Shaun said, kneeling beside him.

Cash blinked away the blurriness and focused on the glass being held up to him.

Shaun pressed it to his lips. "It's water."

"I can hold it," Cash said impatiently and reached for the glass. The liquid was cool on his tongue and a welcome relief. Once he'd drained half the glass he looked around and asked, "Where'd she go?"

"Who? Harlow? She's on her way."

"What? Why?" Cash stared at his brother and then scrambled to his feet as his head pounded. "Ouch. Son of a... What happened here?"

"A ghost attacked you with a board. That's why I called Harlow."

The door slammed below, followed by rapid footsteps as Harlow called out, "Shaun? Where is he?"

Shaun moved to the door and called, "Up here!"

Cash frowned as he ran a hand over the back of his head, finding a small lump. "How long was I out?"

"Too long. Ten minutes maybe?"

"Dammit," Cash muttered. That meant he'd have to go see a healer to check for a concussion.

Harlow appeared, her iron spike in one hand and a pentacle in the other. She stopped abruptly and glanced around the room. After a moment, her concerned gaze landed on Cash. "The spirit's gone. Did it leave on its own or did you send it back to the shadows?"

"She left on her own," he said and closed his eyes, trying to keep the room from spinning.

"She?" Shaun and Harlow asked at the same time.

Then Harlow added, "Was it your ghost stalker?"

"No, that would have been more preferrable, I think," Cash said, moving to lean against the wall. "At least she's never attacked me with a board."

Harlow's eyes widened as she quickly moved to Cash's side and ran a gentle hand over his head.

Cash stiffened at her touch, but then warmth spread through his body and the ache in his breastbone disappeared once more. He stood still, watching as she inspected every inch of his skull until she found the lump and scowled. He took a step back. "I'll need to get to the healer."

"Definitely." She turned to Shaun. "Can you take him to town? I'll do my best to cleanse this place and get a protection circle in place."

"Sure."

Shaun was already moving toward the door when Cash said, "Neither will work."

Harlow, who was already pulling bundles of sage out of her bag, paused and looked up at Cash. "Why not?"

"The ghost is my great-aunt. The house is hers," Cash said.

Harlow dropped the sage back into her bag. No explanation beyond that was needed. When someone died in their home, the only way to get them to move on was for them to do so willingly. They could ask, but Aunt Jane wouldn't be swayed by sage or salt circles. In fact, he'd already done both before he'd moved in and was surprised Harlow had just assumed he hadn't.

"Okay," Harlow said, rubbing her temple. "Any idea why your aunt attacked you?"

He knew exactly why, but he'd be damned if he was going to tell her. No matter how misguided, his aunt had been trying to get them in the same room to try to play matchmaker. Maybe she thought that if they spoke they'd work things out. But Cash knew better. He'd spent the last few months dropping in down at Equinox and that hadn't changed anything. "Maybe she didn't like the fact that we're doing renovations. You know how ghosts get when their homes are in upheaval."

Harlow's shoulders relaxed. "If that's the case, you know what to do." She lifted her bag onto her shoulder and moved toward the door. Immediately, that ice-cold wind picked up again, but instead of boards flying, the bedroom door slammed shut so hard it rattled the walls. The wind vanished and the room went silent again.

"That certainly was a statement," Harlow said as she tried to pull the door open. It wouldn't budge, and she made a face. "Oh, just perfect."

"Now what? Are we supposed to put the damaged boards back to get her to let us out?" Shaun asked.

Cash chuckled softly. The situation was just so absurd he couldn't help himself.

Harlow raised an eyebrow, waiting for him to explain.

Dammit, she really did know him too well. He contemplated making up a lie, but then decided there was no point. What difference would it make anyway? Aunt Jane wasn't likely to stop harassing them until she got what she wanted.

"Cash," Harlow said with both hands on her hips. "What aren't you telling us?"

He leaned against the wall and then slid down so that he was sitting on the subfloor. "Aunt Jane did all of this to get you here," he said to Harlow. "She said we need to work our stuff out."

"Aunt Jane doesn't even know me," Harlow said, looking taken aback. "Does she even know *you*?"

"She does now. I've been living here for months." He sounded tired even to his own ears. "Besides, does that matter? If she watched our show, she'd know we were partners." *In every sense of the word*, he thought, but he didn't add that.

"Right." It was Harlow's turn to sound tired. "What does she want us to do? Rehash why we broke up?"

"Maybe." Cash let out a long sigh.

Shaun glanced back and forth between them and finally said, "You know, I'd really like to know what happened myself."

The door swung open, and Imogen walked in. She stood in the doorway, her face frozen with fear as she scanned the room. She was holding a cross with one hand and a sachet of what Cash assumed was herbs in the other. She held the items out, moving in a semi-circle as if to ward off any evil. It was only when she spotted Harlow standing near Cash that relief shone from her dark eyes. "I got worried."

Harlow hurried to move toward her, but as soon as she moved, the icy wind picked up again, holding her in place.

Imogen let out a scream of terror and tried to run toward her sister, but there seemed to be some sort of barrier that kept her from getting closer than ten feet to either Cash or Harlow.

"Stop!" Harlow cried. "Aunt Jane, that's enough. You're terrifying my sister."

The wind died down immediately, but the door slammed closed again.

"Harlow?" Imogen asked, her voice shaking. "What's happening?"

"Cash's Aunt Jane appears to be upset that Cash and I broke up, and she engineered a plan for us to get in the room together to talk it out. Now we're stuck here until we hash it out, I guess."

Imogen blinked a few times and then turned her focus to Cash. "Your Aunt Jane is upset you're not with Harlow anymore?"

"It would appear so," he said. "Looks like she might be looking for an explanation. Or a reconciliation. Not sure. All I know is she knocked me out and got Shaun to call Harlow, and now here we are."

Imogen's expression went from terror to pure fury. "Seriously, Aunt Jane?" she yelled. "You think it's okay to just interfere in someone's life like that? Well, I'll tell you exactly what happened. I hope you're ready for this." Imogen paced around the room, her arms flailing as she said, "It all started when some witch of a ghost was pissed at Harlow and decided to use me to get back at her."

"I didn't know this part," Shaun said quietly.

Imogen glanced at Shaun, the fury in her expression

disappearing for just a moment when she said in a quiet voice, "It's not something I talk about."

Shaun nodded once.

"What are you doing here?" she asked him curiously.

"I got the feeling it was where I was needed." He winked at her, and Cash couldn't help wondering what the hell that was about. They knew each other, obviously, but Shaun and Imogen hadn't been particularly close.

"You could have told me the details, you know," Shaun said, giving Cash an accusing glare.

Cash gave him an apologetic look. It was true, he hadn't told Shaun everything. He'd been too upset after everything went down to get into the minutiae of what had happened.

"Harlow and Cash were hired to eradicate a ghost that was haunting a giant estate out in Virginia. The property was worth a crazy amount, but so was the jewelry and art collection that was left to the family. Buyers kept getting scared off by the spirit who didn't want to let any of it go. It just so happened that I was with Harlow one day when she was there trying to banish it. She wasn't having any success, because as luck would have it, the ghost was like the one spirit that never reveals itself to Harlow. She couldn't see it and only knew it was there when it was so agitated it put off some sort of vibe that made Harlow sick to her stomach. Anyway, Harlow tried everything she could to get that spirit back into the shadows, only in the end, the spirit found a way to possess me."

Shaun winced. "That's horrifying."

Both Harlow and Cash nodded.

"Oh, yeah," Imogen confirmed. "But Harlow had no idea. And over the next few months, that spirit overtook my entire being. She made me mean and spiteful, spent all my money on crazy expensive stuff like lavish spa days and four-hundred-dollar meals. She even rented an apartment overlooking Central Park in New York City. When my money ran out, she started stealing the antiques from the estate and pawning them to fund her over-the-top lifestyle. The entire time, Harlow had no idea it was the spirit and tried to drag me to three different psychiatrists because she was convinced I was having a prolonged manic episode."

"I had no idea what was really going on," Harlow said quietly.

"That's right," Imogen said, sounding defiant. "My own sister believed that I was mentally ill. The one who had been fighting spirits for over ten years. It wasn't until another spirit happened to show up in that Central Park apartment one night when Harlow was there. The ghost called me by another name, and Harlow started to figure it out. It took her another three weeks to finally free me from that Crazy Cora."

"And she almost died doing it," Cash added, his tone full of fury.

"Holy hell," Shaun whispered. "I knew the breakup was a disagreement over ghost hunting, but I had no idea." He reached out and squeezed Imogen's hand. "I can't imagine how terrifying that was."

"No, you can't. That's why I told Harlow that I couldn't be in her life if she was still hunting ghosts, because I never want to go through that again. Or this. So thank you very much, Aunt Jane, but I want off this ride, right now!"

The door swung open very slowly.

"Thank you," Imogen said as her shoulders sagged in relief.

"And that's why you two broke up?" Shaun asked Cash, looking confused. "Because Harlow gave up ghost hunting?"

"Yes... and no," Cash said.

"Yes," Harlow said, her hands on her hips. "Cash wasn't ready to give it up. And I knew that if we stayed together, we'd end up right back here." She waved a hand around the room. "Ghosts wouldn't ever leave us alone if we were together."

"Looks like they aren't leaving you alone while you're apart," Shaun said, stating the obvious.

"I never asked you to break up with Cash," Imogen said to Harlow. "That was your choice and honestly, I think it was a mistake. You can't live your life for me, Harlow. You need to do what's right for you. And I'll do what's right for me." She turned to Shaun. "I'm leaving. Can you give me a ride home while Harlow takes Cash to the healer?"

"I can take you home," Harlow said, already moving toward her sister. "Shaun can take Cash to the healer."

"No," Imogen said, her expression set in stone. "Like I said, I never told you to break up with Cash. You did that, and you haven't been yourself since then. So while I don't care for Aunt Jane's tactics at all, I don't disagree that you two need to work this out. Either get back together or figure out how to be apart without being miserable, because I'm tired of feeling like I ruined your life!"

Cash stared at Imogen, wondering if he'd just heard her correctly as she stormed out of the room.

Shaun glanced at Cash, clearly looking for confirmation that he should go after her.

Cash nodded. "I'll call you when we're done at the healer."

When their siblings were gone, Cash looked at Harlow and said, "So… That was interesting. What will it be, Harlow? Get back together or—"

Before he could finish that sentence, Harlow was right there in front of him, her hands on his cheeks as she claimed his mouth with hers, kissing him with everything she had.

CHAPTER 11

*H*arlow's entire world narrowed to the man in front of her. After an entire year of denying herself the one person she wanted most in the world, all of her resistance had vanished, and she felt like she was finally home.

Cash's arms came around her, and Harlow deepened the kiss, wanting to stay lost in him forever.

But all too soon, Cash gently pulled back, and in a breathless voice he whispered, "Damn, I missed that."

She looked up at him, her pulse racing with both anticipation and fear. There was no denying that she wanted him, wanted to be back in his life and back in his arms forever, but she was also terrified of what that might mean for the future.

Cash reached up and brushed a lock of hair out of her eyes. "As much as I want to do that again, don't you think we should talk about what happened?"

Harlow took a step back, realizing that as long as she was in Cash's arms she was never going to be able to think clearly. Stumbling over one of the discarded floorboards, she went down with a hard *thunk* and winced when she smacked her elbow on the subfloor.

"Careful," Cash said gently, reaching down to help her up. "The last thing we need is both of us with an egg on our noggins."

"Holy hell, Cash," she said, feeling like an idiot. "Here I am supposed to be taking you to the healer, and I jumped you instead." She kept a tight grip on his hand and started to tug him toward the door. "Let's get going before it gets any later."

"Hold on." He held still and pulled her back toward him until she was standing in front of him again. "Just to be clear, I'd go through another dozen whacks on the head if it meant I'd get another kiss like that."

She gave him an are-you-kidding-me look and rolled her eyes. "Seriously? You could have a concussion."

"I could. I could also be hallucinating this right now, but if I am, I'm not interested in returning to reality. It's been hell living here in Keating Hollow, knowing you're just a few miles away and not being able to be with you. All I want is for you to tell me that we'll find a way to work this out."

"I wish I could, Cash. You know that. But I just can't go back to the way things were before."

"I never said we had to go back to that life," he said gently.

"You weren't ready to give it up a year ago," she countered.

"But I did it anyway, didn't I?" He glanced around the room. "What do you think I've been doing since I settled here?"

"Torturing me?"

He chuckled. "Is that what I was doing?"

"Yes," she admitted. "How was I supposed to move on with you here in Keating Hollow?"

"You weren't supposed to," he said, his eyes flashing with jealousy. "I knew that the moment I realized we'd somehow ended up in the same town, hundreds of miles from Ojai. What we have, Harlow, it's forever. We both know it. We just have to figure out how to make it work. I have faith. Do you?"

She didn't know if she did, but she nodded anyway, desperate for it to work out between them.

"Good. Now take me to the healer so they can put a stop to this massive headache that's forming behind my eyes."

"Right." Harlow turned and led the way out of the house as Cash kept a tight grip on her hand all the way to the Mustang.

"Celia," Cash said, running a hand over the fender of the car. "I've missed you, too."

"You can flirt with her later," Harlow said, opening the passenger door for him. "After we see the healer."

"You're not jealous?" Cash asked, forcing a smile.

Harlow stared at his narrowed eyes and the strained expression on his face and frowned. There was no doubt he was struggling with the pain. "Just get in, Cash. I'll worry about the car stealing your heart later."

He did as she said, and they headed into town.

THE OLD FARMHOUSE was dark when Harlow pulled into the driveway two hours later. The healer had confirmed Cash had a mild concussion, gave him a potion to help both the concussion and his headache, and told them someone needed to watch him through the night to make sure his symptoms didn't get any worse. Cash had said that was no problem. His brother would be home.

But there was no sign of him now.

"Is Shaun still with Imogen?" Harlow asked, noting that the only vehicle she saw was Cash's Jeep.

"Maybe?" Cash pulled his phone out and called his brother. "There's no answer."

Harlow killed the engine of the Mustang, fumbled around for her phone, and hit Imogen's name. "She's not answering either." A trickle of fear started to work its way through Harlow's consciousness, and she took a deep breath, trying to calm herself. Ever since her sister's possession last year, Harlow hadn't been able to shake the anxiety that paralyzed her every time she couldn't reach her sister.

"Let's check the house," Cash said. "Make sure Shaun isn't here. It wouldn't be the first time he's fooled me into thinking no one was home."

"What? Why would he do that?" Harlow asked as she scrambled after him.

"Something about waiting to see if his vision came true, I think. I'm not sure. Better to just check."

The pair of them searched every room of the house, including the one Aunt Jane had used to trap them. Thankfully, there wasn't any more activity from her. Their search came up empty, and as they were on their way back outside, Cash tried Shaun again.

"Nope." He climbed back into the Mustang. "Chances are high he went to go get a beer or something. I'm sure he'll be back. Let's just go check on Imogen and make sure she made it home okay."

"I just don't know why she isn't answering her phone. She knows how worried I get," Harlow said, trying to shut down all the horrific scenarios that were flashing through her mind. Had Crazy Cora returned? The spirit had just reappeared yesterday on the solstice. Harlow had been fairly sure she'd be sent back into the shadows after the sun rose due to the salt circle she'd trapped her in, but what if she hadn't? It wasn't as if Harlow had gone back to her old apartment to check.

She mentally berated herself as she flew down the country roads of Keating Hollow. Why hadn't she warned Imogen that the spirit had appeared? She knew why. She hadn't wanted to scare her. She hadn't wanted to rock the boat.

But that had been stupid if not downright dangerous. Even though Harlow had done her best to protect their new house, Imogen wouldn't be protected from the spirit when she was out and about in Keating Hollow. She shouldn't have just assumed everything would be fine. Especially since that spirit had a connection to Imogen.

But she had her pentacle and her herbs that Harlow had given her last year. Both were helpful with repelling unwelcome spirits. Though Harlow knew if one was determined enough, there wasn't much an inexperienced witch could do if the spirit wanted to haunt someone.

"Harlow," Cash said quietly.

"Huh?" She glanced over at him, tightening her grip on the steering wheel.

He gave her a small smile. "Breathe."

"I'm breathing," she said as air rushed out of her lungs.

"Barely. Just don't worry yourself to death until there's something to worry about, okay?"

"I can't help it," she said and concentrated on filling her lungs with air. "She never ignores my calls. Not for this long. She knows how I worry."

"Chances are she's still with Shaun and they're out getting a drink or something."

"Yeah, I hope so." Still, Harlow couldn't help the dread that was coiling in her gut. "If something happens to her…"

Cash reached over and squeezed her shoulder. "Everything

will be okay. Shaun wouldn't let anything happen to her. You'll see."

Harlow just nodded, praying he was right.

When they arrived at Harlow's rented house, she parked behind her Subaru and peered at the unfamiliar gray truck. "Please tell me that's Shaun's truck."

"It is. I told you they were together somewhere," Cash said with a nod.

Harlow raised both eyebrows. "But why aren't they answering their phones? It doesn't make sense." She climbed out of the car and rushed over to the Subaru to grab her backpack of ghost-hunting tricks. Without saying a word, she handed an iron chain to Cash. "Be ready."

"You really think we're walking into something involving a spirit?" he asked as he admired the chain. Then he held it up and said, "Thank you for this. I was feeling a little lost without the one I broke yesterday."

"I figured you were. As far as spirit activity goes, you know what I always used to say, expect the unexpected."

He nodded. "That and better to be prepared than knocked on your ass when an angry spirit comes for you."

She snorted. They had always said that. But then she quickly sobered and said, "Let's go."

The house was lit up with light shining from the windows, and Harlow half expected to see Shaun and her sister just sitting on the couch, blissfully ignoring everyone and everything. Or at least that's what she hoped for.

Unfortunately, that wasn't the case. When Harlow stepped through the door, she scanned the abandoned living room, finding nothing but two half-empty wineglasses and a broken plate on the floor.

A chill crawled up her arms, and suddenly her vision

blurred as panic started to take over. Something terrible must have happened.

Cash moved past her into the kitchen. When he returned, he shook his head, indicating he hadn't found anything.

That's when she heard it. A small cry that came from the back of the house.

"This way!" Harlow said in a harsh whisper as she hurried down the hall. To the right, the door was open to Harlow's darkened room. And to the left—a low moan sounded. To Harlow, it sounded like a wounded animal.

Without a second thought, she burst through the door and then froze, her eyes wide as her brain caught up with the scene before her.

"Harlow!" her sister cried, frantically reaching for the sheet to cover her naked body.

Shaun, who'd rolled off Imogen the moment she'd cried her sister's name, muttered a curse under his breath as he placed a pillow over his naked bits.

Cash chuckled softly behind Harlow as he placed both hands on her shoulders. "Looks like they are more than fine. Let's give them some privacy."

"Imogen?" Harlow asked, still in a state of shock.

"Harlow, just go!" Imogen ordered. "Gods, you'd think I was a teenager and my parents just walked in."

"Right." Harlow cleared her throat. "Sorry. Carry on."

"Carry on?" Cash asked as they retreated to the hall. "Seriously?"

Harlow threw her hands up in defeat. "I don't know. I went from thinking that my sister was being tortured to finding out that your brother has a mole on his right butt cheek, just like you do. I was flustered, okay?"

"I did not need to hear about my brother's mole," he said with a groan.

A laugh bubbled out of Harlow's lips. She clamped her hand over her mouth, but there was no stopping the hysterics. The laughter intensified and she doubled over, holding her stomach, unable to control herself.

"Okay, gorgeous, get ahold of yourself," Cash said, his voice full of humor. "Let's get out of here and give them some privacy."

"Wait," Harlow said, gasping for air. "Let me pack an overnight bag. Someone still needs to stay with you tonight. And from the looks of things, it's not going to be Shaun."

He raised an eyebrow. "You're going to stay the night with me?"

"Don't read too much into it, Keys," she said, still smiling as she used her nickname for him for the first time in over a year. She'd started calling him that when she'd learned he was the keyboardist in a bad metal band back in his high school days.

He grinned. "Keys?"

"Don't read into that either." Harlow disappeared into her bedroom, and after a few minutes, she met him outside. Instead of taking the Mustang, she waved him over to the Subaru.

"I prefer Celia," he said as he pulled the passenger door open.

"I'm sure you do, but it's Imogen's car now, and I'm certainly not going back in there to ask if I can keep borrowing it. My eyes are already due for a good bleaching."

He laughed. "Fair point."

CHAPTER 12

"*H*ave you eaten dinner yet?" Harlow asked as she swept into Cash's house and dropped her overnight bag near the front door.

"No. Nothing since lunch, but I'm not really that hungry," Cash said.

"You have to eat something. I'll whip something up for you, and in the meantime, you go lie down. I'll bring it to you."

Cash ignored her order and followed her into the kitchen, unwilling to be too far from her. He'd missed her, missed this *easiness* between them too much. He'd craved her company for far too long. Retreating to another room wasn't an option.

"Cash," she said, sounding impatient when she realized he was still behind her. "You're supposed to be resting. You heard what Healer Whipple said."

"She said I wasn't supposed to do anything like exercise or exert any effort that would get my heart rate up. Or drive, read, or watch television. I'm doing none of those things," he said, taking a seat at the kitchen table just to appease her. The truth was that ever since the healer had given him that potion, he'd felt fine. The goose egg on his skull had even gone down significantly.

"She said you were supposed to rest for at least the next twenty-four hours. That means lying down," she insisted.

"You didn't mind when I went with you to check on your sister," he challenged.

She pressed her lips together into a thin line, and he watched as the muscle ticked in her jaw.

His smile widened. He knew he had her. She'd forgotten all about the healer's instructions when she'd thought Imogen was in danger. "Sitting at the table is far better than bouncing around in a vehicle, don't you think?"

"You're impossible," she said, shaking her head. "Just sit there and look pretty."

"Gladly." Cash leaned back in the chair and watched her as she buzzed around the kitchen as if she owned the place. It was remarkable how she just seemed to know where to find whatever she was looking for. She was as comfortable in his kitchen as she had been in the house they'd shared in Ojai. He eyed the pot she'd set on the stove. "What are you making?"

"Looks like chicken pasta with a small salad. I didn't see any rice, otherwise I'd have made a stir fry," she said, giving him a flat, judgmental stare.

"Fresh out of rice," he quipped.

She snorted. "Sure. You expect me to believe you actually made yourself rice?"

He shrugged one shoulder, remaining noncommittal. They both knew he hadn't made any rice. For some reason he had a mental block when it came to using a rice cooker, and every time he'd tried in the past, it had either come out crunchy or so soft that it resembled mush. He'd given up trying long ago. Pasta was just easier.

"One of these days, all that pasta is going to catch up with you, Cash," she said, turning the burner on.

"Not today. In fact, Healer Whipple said it was best to load up on carbs. She said it would help my brain heal faster."

"She did say that, and that's why I'm making pasta." Harlow filled a glass of water from the pitcher in the refrigerator and set it in front of him. "Don't forget to hydrate."

"Thanks, gorgeous." He winked and took a long sip of the cool liquid. As Harlow worked on making his dinner, Cash said, "Tell me about working at Equinox."

"What do you want to know?" she asked, glancing over at him, a small frown on her face. "I run the place, but I'm mostly just a glorified bartender."

"I'm sure you do more than that. But what I really want to know is why you're working there at all." He knew she had more than enough money to live on for years to come. They both did.

"To keep my mind busy," she said, not looking at him.

He was quiet for a long moment as he took that in. "I see."

Harlow met his gaze, her eyes searching his. "And what have you been doing for the past year, Cash?"

He shifted in his seat, suddenly uncomfortable under her piercing gaze. "Well, for the past few months, I've spent most of my time settling Aunt Jane's estate and then working on fixing up this house."

"And before that?" She was careful to keep her tone light, but Cash saw right through her and knew what she was really asking.

He could lie. Say that he'd considered a number of different career options. Or even say that he drank away a few months on a beach, mending his broken heart, but that was no way to rebuild a relationship. If he wanted things to work out with Harlow, he knew he had to be honest.

"After you left town, I spent a few months talking to every studio head I could get a meeting with, trying to pitch a new show," he said, staring at his fingertips that were strumming the tabletop.

"I heard," she said quietly. When he looked up, startled, she grimaced. "My agent told me. Actually, she begged me to consider some of the offers."

"Offers?" Cash sat up straighter. "You had offers?"

She blinked. "You didn't know? I thought..." Harlow shook her head, looking confused.

"You thought what?" Cash asked, feeling like he'd missed something important. Something that might have changed everything. When she didn't elaborate, Cash said, "Harlow, please. Can't we just be honest? Can't we at least give each other that much?"

Tears filled her eyes, but she quickly blinked them back as she nodded. "Yes, we can do that." Then she wiped her hands on a dishtowel and came to sit next to him at the table. She placed her hands in her lap and looked up to meet his gaze. "About a month after we split, I came to see you."

"What?" He felt that ache in this chest return, and he unconsciously rubbed at it. "You did?"

"I did. You weren't home, so I left you a note in the mailbox, asking you to call me. I wanted to talk things out, see if we could try something not ghost-related maybe. I mean, offers were coming in, I thought maybe we could get a studio on board with a new angle. I was thinking something like home improvement or a talk show. But really, I was thinking about maybe launching a true-stories type of show. Invite other people in to tell their unexplained mysteries and phenomena.

They were just ideas, but then when you never got in touch, I thought maybe you were too mad at the fact that I walked away and—"

"I never got your note," Cash rushed out as he reached for her hand. "I would have called."

"You didn't? I put it in an envelope and everything," Harlow said, and her brow furrowed. "Does that mean someone took it?"

"I don't know," he said, shaking his head. "Maybe? I guess it's possible I dropped it when grabbing the mail. One thing's for certain; I would have called."

She blew out a long breath. "I was surprised you didn't take any of the deals the studios were offering."

Cash let out a humorless bark of laughter. "Harlow, they didn't offer *me* anything. They all wanted to know if you were part of the negotiations, and when I said no, they ghosted my agent."

Harlow's mouth opened into a shocked *O*. "You can't be serious. That's… insane. Why?"

Cash gave her a rueful smile. "Because you're the face their male demographic was tuning in to watch while our relationship was apparently the draw for our female audience."

"But…" She trailed off then closed her eyes and ignored the nausea in her gut. "That explains the offers they were sending my way."

"What did they offer?" Cash leaned forward, intensely curious. "Paranormal Island Investigations? Investigations Down Under? Traveling Haunted Cities?" They were all variations of their show *Paranormal in a Small Town*, but it was Cash's experience that the studios never wanted to try anything that was too far from their former successes.

"Um, no. It was more like Haunting Love Island and The Haunted Bachelorette."

He stared at her, stunned. "They wanted you to do a haunted dating show?"

She nodded slowly. "They also suggested having the two of us spend a month in a haunted house and film it sort of like *Big Brother*. That was the one I thought you might be interested in, only without me of course."

"Of course." Cash knew why they didn't contact him with that idea. For Cash and Harlow, the work had always come first. They prided themselves on helping people either connect with lost loved ones or ridding spaces of unsavory spirits. The network, however, was more interested in the relationship between Cash and Harlow. Without her, there was no show. But they were likely willing to give her a contract if she'd agree to share the space with some other male who the public could see as a love interest.

"Cash, I—" Harlow started, but he cut her off.

"That's all in the past now, gorgeous. Can we just focus on what's here in front of us?"

"And what's that?" she asked, trepidation in her tone.

"You and me. A new life here in Keating Hollow. Focusing on us instead of a career," he said hopefully.

"Do you really think we can do that?" she asked, her brow furrowed.

"We can try." He took her hand in his and lightly caressed her palm. "It's what we've been doing apart. I don't see why we can't do it together."

"I want to say yes." Tears shone in Harlow's eyes again, but she didn't let them fall. "I'm just concerned that if we're together the spirits will never leave us alone."

Her fears were valid. They'd spent so many years inviting ghosts into their world that eventually the ones who wanted to talk just showed up, somehow knowing they had an audience who would listen. It had happened to each of them individually, but it was far more common when they were together. It was as if their collective energy had become a beacon for wayward spirits. "We'll just have to do our best to ward them off. I imagine if we stay closed off they'll eventually leave us alone, don't you think?"

Harlow let out a huff of sardonic laughter. "Sure, Cash. I think we have as much chance of that as we do winning the lottery."

"I'm game if you are," he said and then held his breath.

She let out a long sigh, stared at him with her piercing golden-brown eyes, and then nodded. "I want to try. But Cash?"

"Yeah?" he asked, willing to grant her just about anything she wanted.

"If it ends up like last time, with spirits never leaving us alone, I don't know if I can deal with that. Not now. Not after what happened to Imogen."

"Then I hope we find a way to ward them off, because you've got the other half of my heart, Harlow Thane. You always have, and you always will."

She stood and moved to stand right next to him.

Cash got to his feet, wrapped his arms around her, pulling her close, and pressed his lips to hers, putting all of his hopes and dreams into the slow and tender kiss.

Harlow melted into him, hugging him so tight it was a little hard to breathe.

And when she deepened the kiss, things progressed from sweet to a little bit heated. Cash chuckled softly and pulled back just enough to break their connection. "I'm not supposed to be exerting too much effort, remember?"

Harlow gave him a sheepish smile. "I guess I got carried away."

"I'm not complaining." Then he kissed her again, this time burying a hand in her hair as he showed her exactly how much he'd missed her.

All thought of the healer's instructions fled from his mind as his world reduced to just Harlow and her soft, sweet taste. He wanted to claim her, remind her exactly who she belonged to with just the use of his mouth. But when the buzzer on the stove started to beep, they broke apart with both of their lips slightly swollen and their cheeks flushed.

"I think that might be enough of that," Harlow said with a nervous laugh as she moved back to the stove to deal with the pasta. "Until tomorrow, anyway."

Cash sat back down, and despite his concussion, he felt whole for the first time in over a year.

CHAPTER 13

"No, I'm not sleeping in here," Harlow said with a nervous chuckle. "You have to rest."

Cash, who was standing just inside his bedroom door, tightened his grip on her hand and tugged her a little closer. "But then you'll have to get up multiple times to check on me. Wouldn't it be easier if you just slept here and set an alarm? Then you can just roll over and make sure I'm still breathing."

"With my luck, you'll be rolling on top of me all night," she said, shaking her head, even as her body screamed for her to give in to his request. Every night since they'd separated, she'd missed the weight of his body next to her at night, the sound of his breathing, the knowledge that he was right there next to her when she needed him. But it had been well over a year since they'd been together, and that meant she didn't trust either one of them to follow the healer's orders. "I know you, Cash Moses. You won't be able to keep your hands to yourself."

"What if I promise to behave?" he asked, trying and failing to look innocent.

Harlow let out a loud laugh. "You're a terrible liar, Cash. You're going to have to hold off for one more night."

"Damn," he muttered under his breath, and without waiting for her to leave his room, he tugged his shirt off.

Harlow's gaze landed on his well sculpted pecs and then moved to his six pack abs, and she couldn't help the little gasp she let out.

Cash's lips twitched into a self-satisfied smile.

"You're evil," she said, and although she knew she should retreat, give him privacy to get ready for bed, her feet seemed to be glued to the floor.

It wasn't until his hands went to the fly of his jeans and he started to undo the top button that she finally took a step back and said, "I'll be back in a couple of hours to... ah..." She couldn't tear her gaze away from his hands as he slowly lowered the zipper on his jeans.

"To do what, Harlow?" he asked, sliding his pants over his hips, leaving him in just his black boxer briefs.

"Um..." She licked her lips, knowing she was making a fool of herself. She was hot all over and her fingers twitched to start stripping her own body of her clothes.

Cash draped his jeans over a chair near the bed and then took a step closer to her. He reached out and brushed her long dark hair off her shoulder and said, "You're still here. Does that mean you're going to stay?"

"No. Nope," she said suddenly and spun on her heel. "I'll be back. Just... get some rest."

He was still laughing to himself as she shut the door and then just stood there, sucking in air.

"Evil," she whispered as she pressed a hand to her chest, trying and failing to get her heartrate under control. At least she knew she'd made the right choice in deciding it was best not to sleep in the same room. Although at this rate, she thought she might be the one who couldn't control herself instead of Cash.

Goddess above, that man was gorgeous. She didn't know how she'd found the willpower to leave his room, but she had, and now she needed a cold shower. Or else she might just find herself back in his room, unable to keep her hands to herself.

HARLOW STARED up at the shadows on the ceiling, listening to what sounded like footsteps on the wooden floors. The old house had periodically been making settling noises all night. And ever since she'd settled in on the couch, she couldn't stop wondering if the noises were actually Aunt Jane or some other spirit. It was making it so that even when she nodded off she woke right back up, her ears straining for any strange sounds.

She'd never get any rest at that rate.

It was just past two in the morning, and she'd already visited Cash twice. She'd woken him up, checked to be sure his eyes weren't dilated, and then quickly retreated so that she wouldn't be tempted to crawl into bed with him. Goddess knew, he wasn't making it easy on her. The last trip up there, he'd been lying in only his boxer briefs with the covers kicked off him. His gorgeous body was even more muscular than she remembered, and she wondered if he'd stepped up his workout routine.

Then he'd opened his sleepy eyes and given her that sexy half smile as he tugged her until she was sitting right next to him. His body heat and familiar scent had almost lured her into staying right there, but when his hand started to roam over her thigh, she'd jumped up and retreated back to the couch and the sounds that kept her wide awake.

Harlow had never been afraid of ghosts before. When she was a kid, spirits had shown up regularly to talk to her and she'd never thought twice about it. In fact, for a while when she was very young, she hadn't even realized they were spirits. They were just people she knew. But eventually it became clear that other people couldn't see her friends, and her grandmother explained that she had a gift.

Spirits had come to her for all different reasons. Some just wanted to talk. Others wanted help finding their loved ones. And then there were the ones who didn't know they'd died and needed someone to help them cross over to the light. Those were the most draining but also the most rewarding.

She was in college when she met Cash. He'd been fascinated with her gift. And while he'd seen his share of ghosts, he'd never opened himself to help them before he met Harlow. Once he'd witnessed her help someone cross to the light, he'd been all in, and suddenly spirits were coming to him for help, too. The show had come about after they'd helped a spirit connect with a loved one who was a studio executive. Not long after, they started filming *Paranormal in a Small Town*, and people came to them for help either to contact a spirit or with clearing their spaces of unwanted spirit activity.

It was exactly what they'd been doing before, only they were on television and being paid for it.

Even when spirits were hard to deal with, Harlow hadn't ever been fazed. No, that had happened after Imogen had been possessed and Harlow had nearly lost her life fighting the spirit. After that, Harlow stopped inviting spirits into her energy. And now, the unknown of what a spirit might do sent a shiver of fear down her spine. What if a random spirit she encountered was stronger than her? What if she herself was possessed or worse?

What would happen to Imogen?

That was why she stayed away from any spirit who tried to seek her help now. She just couldn't forgive herself if another spirit she invited into her life hurt her sister again.

Creak, creak, the floors groaned.

Harlow ground her teeth together and got up once again. This time she made her way to the kitchen and rummaged around in the cabinet until she found a box of her favorite herbal tea.

Her favorite.

In Cash's house.

He didn't drink tea. Or at least he hadn't when they were together. She supposed Shaun might, but the box was still wrapped in plastic and no one had opened it. Had Cash stocked his cabinet with the tea on the off chance she came over one day? She thought it was more than likely, and her heart swelled with love for the man who was sleeping upstairs. Even though she'd walked away from him, he'd never completely given up on her. She'd thought he had when he didn't call after she'd left the note, but she believed him when he said he hadn't received it.

Everything inside of her ached for this thing between them to work out. She'd only been going through the motions of living the past year. Already, after only a few hours of letting him back into her heart, she felt whole again.

Sitting in the kitchen, sipping her tea, Harlow's eyes began to water from fatigue. She should lay back down on the couch and try to get some rest, but when she heard that *creak, creak, creak* again, she knew she'd never drift off. Not when she was listening to see if a spirit was going to end up standing over her.

Maybe she'd feel better if she was upstairs with Cash.

Harlow laughed to herself. Of course she'd feel better. It was the only place she wanted to be. The creaking of the wood floors started again, and that was enough to finally convince herself that if she wanted any sleep at all, she was going to have to face facts. It wasn't going to happen on the couch.

She rose from her chair, set her mug in the sink, and resigned herself to the fact that she needed Cash. Likely more than he needed her in that moment.

Harlow was halfway up the stairs when the wind picked up outside and rattled the windows, making her jump. She froze for just a moment before she ran up the stairs and into Cash's bedroom.

He sat straight up in bed, blinking at her. "What's wrong?"

"Nothing. I… oh hell," she said with a grimace. "Your house is making noises, and it startled me. So if you promise to behave, I think I'd like to sleep in here."

"You don't want me to lie, do you?" he asked, his voice gruff with sleep.

"Stop," she said as she climbed into bed on the other side of him and checked her phone to be sure her alarm was set before placing it on the nightstand.

He laid back down and curled into her, rolling her over so that he was spooning her from behind.

Harlow knew that she should ask him to move and put some distance between them, but instead, she placed her hand over his and closed her eyes. Finally, she was right where she belonged.

CHAPTER 14

*C*ash woke to Harlow's alarm going off at 8:00 am. After waking him up every two hours all night long, it appeared she'd finally crashed so completely that she didn't even hear it. Reaching over her, he grabbed her phone and silenced it.

After checking that she was completely out, he shuffled into his bathroom, took care of business, and then checked his own pupils. There was no sign of any dilation, nor did he have any sort of headache or bump on his head.

Good as new, he thought to himself. Still, while he was on his way downstairs to start the coffee maker, he put in a call to the healer's office to report how his night went.

"That's great news," Healer Whipple said. "It sounds like the potion did its job, and you're free to resume your normal activities."

"That means I can get back to the remodel on my house?" he asked specifically because he knew Harlow would fuss at him.

"Yes, Cash. It's fine. You have no more restrictions. Just pay attention to your body. If you start to get a headache or feel dizzy or anything, stop whatever you're doing and call us. Got it?"

"Got it," he said. "Seems like that potion of yours is a miracle worker. Don't concussions usually take longer to heal?"

"They do if there's no magic involved. Lucky for you, I'm very good at my job," she said and then told him she had a patient waiting.

He ended the call, fixed two mugs of coffee, and headed back upstairs to find Harlow still sound asleep, looking like an angel with a tiny smile claiming her lips. Damn, she was gorgeous. How could he tear himself away when she was lying there so peacefully? Usually by this hour, he was already hard at work on something around the house. But today, as long as Harlow was in his bed, he wasn't going anywhere.

When he finished his coffee, he laid back down, but instead of spooning Harlow the way he had when they'd fallen asleep together, he propped himself up on an elbow and gazed down at her, taking her in. He didn't think he'd ever appreciated a moment more. The sun was spilling in the window and splashing over her face, making her look like a goddess. His fingers twitched to touch her, but he kept them to himself, determined to let her sleep.

"I know you're staring at me," she said so softly he barely heard her.

"How do you know?" he asked, amused.

"I can feel you watching me." She blinked the sleep from her eyes and gazed up at him, her lips curved up just a touch. He loved when she looked at him like that.

Happy. Relaxed. Content.

Cash vowed to wake up to that expression on her face

every day for the rest of his life. He gave in to his temptation and brushed a lock of her mussed hair behind her ear and then let his fingers trail down her cheek. "Good morning."

"Morning." Her gaze locked with his, and it was as if the rest of the world just melted away.

Cash bent down and pressed a soft kiss to her lips as his hand trailed over her shoulder and down her arm. He felt, rather than saw, the gooseflesh that popped out on her skin, and he couldn't help the ripple of satisfaction that ran through him.

She wanted him just as much as he wanted her. There was no doubt about it.

"Cash," she said, reaching for his hand as his fingers started to caress the bare skin of her stomach under her T-shirt.

"Hmm?" he murmured as his lips found her neck.

"Gods," she said with a contented sigh. "That feels amazing, but we can't do this. Your concussion."

"I already got the all-clear from the healer. It's fine," he said roughly, pressing his body against hers.

"Seriously?" she asked with a disbelieving chuckle. "You called the healer to find out if it is okay to get it on?"

"No." His chest rumbled just before he bit down lightly on the nape of her neck. "I called to check in, and when I told her all my symptoms were gone, she lifted all restrictions. Now, what about you? What do you want, gorgeous?"

"You know exactly what I want, Cash," Harlow said, letting out a tiny moan when his hand inched up over her breast.

He did, in fact, know what she wanted. Cash knew every inch of her body and exactly what she needed. It had been far too long, and every molecule in his body craved her. His body pulsed with need, and he had to fight the urge to rip her clothes off and waste no time making her his again. But he didn't. He was going to savor this. Rediscover her and show her how much he loved her.

And he did exactly that. Each kiss was a declaration of love, each touch a promise of devotion, and when he finally took her, his eyes were locked on hers, sharing an intensity he'd never experienced before.

Finally, she was his and he was hers again, mind, body, and soul.

CASH WAS WHISTLING to himself when he finally made his way downstairs again. He'd just left Harlow in the shower with the promise of feeding her. They'd spent a few hours in bed, making love twice and just enjoying holding each other. When Harlow's stomach finally grumbled, he'd taken her to the shower and then made love to her again. He just couldn't get enough of her.

When he'd teased her about a fourth round, she'd laughed and shooed him out of the shower, insisting he get her food before she passed out. He'd finally relented but left her with one last searing kiss.

The house was full of sunlight streaming in, and the scent of spring was in the air. Cash felt like a new man as he pulled eggs and bacon out of the refrigerator. He'd just cracked his second egg when he spotted movement out of the corner of his eye.

On reflex, he pulled the iron chain that Harlow had given him out of his pocket and whirled, ready to trap any spirit that had invaded their sanctuary.

"Whoa!" Shaun cried, holding his hands up and backing away. "I come in peace."

"Damn, Shaun. You could have warned a guy you were here," Cash said, stuffing the chain back into his jeans pocket.

"What?" Shaun asked as he pulled two small earbuds from his ears that Cash hadn't noticed.

"I said you could have warned a guy," Cash repeated. "I thought you were still with Imogen."

"Nope. I've been here for a few hours, actually," he said, neatly sidestepping the fact that he'd spent the night with Harlow's sister. He glanced toward the doorway that led to the stairs and then back at Cash. "I guess things with Harlow are back on track?"

"You could say that," Cash said, turning his attention back to his eggs.

"Then I'll invest in some noise-canceling headphones until we can soundproof the bedrooms," Shaun said with a chuckle. "Imagine my horror when I heard Harlow crying out your name."

Cash *tsked*, not at all embarrassed. In fact, he stood taller, basking in the ego rush. "At least you weren't treated to the sight of your brother's hairy ass."

Shaun sputtered. "My ass is *not* hairy."

"How do you know? Have you checked lately? From where I was standing, it looked like you could use a little manscaping," Cash taunted.

"You're full of—" Shaun started.

Harlow appeared in the doorway and cut him off when she cleared her throat.

"Oh, uh, good morning, Harlow," Shaun said, his face turning bright red.

"Shaun," she muttered and then glanced away as she added, "Have a good night?"

He coughed and muttered a *yes*.

"Are the two of you dating now?" Harlow asked pointedly.

"That's, um, not something we've discussed," he said, sounding nervous.

"So last night was... what? A one-night stand? Friends with benefits? A hookup with potential?" Harlow didn't sound mad, not to Cash at least. More like concerned.

"Last night..." Shaun shook his head. "You know what? I'm not comfortable discussing this. I'm sorry, Harlow, I know Imogen is your sister, but what happens between us is *between us*. If you want to know more, you'll have to ask her." Then he turned and quickly exited the kitchen.

Cash frowned as he watched his brother. While he agreed that whatever was between Imogen and Shaun was their business, he also got the feeling that Shaun was struggling with something. He just prayed it wasn't regret. Having his brother at odds with Imogen would be a complication none of them needed.

"Hey, babe," Cash said, walking over to Harlow and giving her a kiss on the temple. "I'm working on breakfast now. Give me about twenty minutes and we'll be good to go."

She looked up at him, her expression softening as she glanced at the stove and then back at him. "Would you be too upset if I took a raincheck? I want to get home and make sure Imogen is all right."

He raised his eyebrows in question. "You're worried about her and Shaun?"

"Aren't you?" she asked.

"I don't know that worried is the word, but I am curious about what is going on. Shaun hasn't dated anyone since he and his fiancée broke up."

"He just said they aren't dating," she said, her expression troubled. "I know hookups are a thing and they're both adults.

They don't need to answer to me. And I know that Shaun's a good guy. It's just that Imogen isn't the one-night-stand kind of girl and I… I don't know. There's nothing wrong with that, but it's not her personality, and that worries me. And what about Shaun? I've never known him to be a hit-it-and-quit-it type of guy. Have you?"

Cash averted his gaze and frowned.

"Oh no," Harlow said.

"It's not that bad. It's not like he's been parading hookups around. In fact, I haven't seen him with anyone since Shari, but he did just confirm yesterday that he's not a monk, so I took that to mean that he's definitely shared a bed or two."

Harlow groaned. "I don't want to talk about our siblings' sex lives. It's too weird."

He chuckled. "I agree." Then he sobered and pulled her in close. "Will I see you tonight?"

"Sorry," she said, giving him an apologetic smile. "I have a girls' night planned with Hanna from the café, and Imogen is coming along. Tomorrow?"

"Count on it." He gave her one more long, lingering kiss and then walked her out.

As he watched her Subaru disappear out of his driveway, he had the intense urge to follow her. Instead, he turned around and went back into his house, already mentally making plans for their future.

CHAPTER 15

*H*arlow pulled her Subaru into the driveway next to the blue Mustang and took a deep breath before heading into the house. After walking in on Imogen and Shaun, Harlow dreaded the awkwardness and the necessary conversation she knew that Imogen wouldn't want to have.

There was just no way around it. Harlow was in a no-win situation. If Imogen was acting out of character, Harlow had no choice but to question everything. After last year's fiasco, how could she not?

The house was quiet and smelled like pine cleaner. The wine glasses and the broken plate from the night before had been cleared, and the coffee table shined as if Imogen had dusted.

Harlow smiled to herself. As far as roommates went, she could do worse. "Imogen?" she called as she walked into the kitchen. The sink was empty, and the counters gleamed. But Imogen didn't answer her call and was nowhere to be found. After quickly checking the rest of the house, she found Imogen's bedroom door open, the bed made, and the only thing out of place was a notebook that had been left on her bed.

Frowning, Harlow retreated back to the living room and then eventually outside. It was a gorgeous spring day. Maybe she was outside tinkering in the neglected garden.

No such luck. Harlow was just about to text Imogen when she heard a rustling coming from the woods just behind the house. She looked up just in time to see Imogen emerge from the trees carrying a tote bag on one shoulder. "Hey, where've you been?" Harlow asked.

"Out at the waterfall, taking advantage of magical energy." Imogen swept past her and entered the house through the back door.

"Wait, what?" Harlow called as she hurried after her sister. "What were you doing dabbling with magical energy?"

"I *am* a witch," Imogen said dismissively as she reached into the tote and placed the white pillar candles onto the kitchen table. A familiar journal that had belonged to their grandmother followed, along with a bag of assorted herbs.

"Of course you are," Harlow said, more confused than ever. "But you've repeatedly told me that you don't want to have anything to do with magic or ghosts."

"I know what I said. I'm allowed to change my mind, aren't I?"

"Well, yes, but what changed?"

She shrugged. "I guess being in Keating Hollow yesterday and seeing the charming magic of the town has convinced me that not all magic is bad. Besides, these spells don't have anything to do with ghosts." Imogen opened the journal and flipped to the middle of the book. Holding it out for Harlow she said, "If I'm going to hang out my shingle to be a wedding planner, I'm going to need to brush up on some of these enchantment spells."

"Yesterday you said that if I was going to be involved with ghosts when I was needed that you were going to have to move. Did you change your mind on that, too?" Harlow asked, feeling as if she were completely out of the loop. None of what Imogen was saying made sense to her.

Imogen waved a hand as if dismissing the comment. "I said that in the heat of the moment. Obviously, you have to help if you're needed. I just don't want to be a part of it. So the sooner I get my business up and running, the sooner I can get my own place. Then you can do your thing and I'll do mine."

Harlow bit down on her bottom lip, wondering exactly what that meant. "So what are you saying? That once you move out we won't be in each other's lives anymore?"

"Don't be so dramatic, Harlow," Imogen said, rolling her eyes. "I just don't want to be around when you're dealing with ghosts. That will be easier if I have my own space."

"Okay, good." Harlow let out a long breath as the tension drained from her shoulders. It was a fact that Imogen had been helping Harlow at the estate when that ghost possessed her. Maybe this new plan would be just the thing to help them both move forward in their lives.

Harlow scanned the spell in question. It was an old one that charmed butterflies to behave on command, and it had been passed down through the family for generations. It was primarily used during a celebration when the spell caster wanted the butterflies to hang around on something like flowers growing on an arbor. Then they were released during a toast or when the newlyweds departed for their honeymoon. Harlow had seen it used a few times, and the effect was beautiful. Harlow looked up at her sister. "Did you get it to work?"

"Sure," she said with a nod. "There were two butterflies that came when I called to them, and then they seemed happy to move from flower to flower until I thanked them and released them from the spell. The best part is that they both hung around for a while. One even landed on my finger and fluttered her wings for a few moments to show off her electric-blue coloring."

"I wish I'd been there for that," Harlow said, moving into the kitchen to finally make herself something to eat. She grabbed a glass of orange juice and then turned to her sister. "Are you hungry? I'm going to make waffles and maybe some bacon if we have any."

Imogen glanced at the clock. It was already past twelve. "You haven't had breakfast yet? Don't the Moses boys keep any food in that house?"

A weird energy passed between them when Imogen mentioned Cash and Shaun.

Harlow took a long sip of the juice and then cleared her throat. "Yes, they do. Cash was going to make me some breakfast, but I decided I'd rather eat here with you and catch up on the past twenty-four hours."

Imogen rolled her eyes. "There's nothing to catch up on. You already know more details than you should. Can't we just let this go?"

"I want to, trust me," Harlow said, "but it just isn't like you to have a one-night stand."

"I'm twenty-eight years old, Harlow. I don't think we need to be having this discussion." Imogen slapped the journal closed. "Are you going to question everything I do for the rest of my life?"

Again, there was a long silence before Harlow said, "No. But after what happened last year, I just need to make sure I'm not missing anything again. That the ghost hasn't come back and—"

"Possessed me?" Imogen asked, her voice ice cold. "That's ludicrous, Harlow. I'm hardly acting like Crazy Cora. I'd think my own sister could tell the difference."

"Imogen, please don't get upset. I just wanted to check in with you to make sure there's nothing to worry about."

"There's nothing to worry about, okay? Now you can stop judging me for sleeping with Shaun." She started putting her candles back in the tote.

"I'm not judging you, Gen," Harlow said softly. "I just don't want to make the same mistakes I made last year. With Shaun staying over and you doing magic today, can't you at least see that both of those things are out of character for you? At least from my perspective."

Imogen ground her teeth together. "I already told you why I was practicing magic. Doing harmless spells is hardly going to invite a crazytown ghost into my orbit. Cora would in no way be interested in butterflies or fireflies or the dancing gnomes."

"Dancing gnomes?" Harlow asked, trying to picture a scenario where a bride would want animated gnomes.

"I saw it on a wedding blog, okay? People are into all kinds of things," she said, waving a hand. "Forget the gnomes. And as far as Shaun goes, if you must know, last night was not a one-night stand. Are you happy now?"

Harlow blinked, trying to process her sister's words. "Are you dating Shaun?"

"No... yes... I don't know." She shook her head. "Again, this isn't your business, Harlow. Why can't you just let me live my life?"

"Because the last time I did that, you were possessed by a ghost. And when I didn't realize it, you blamed me for not doing anything!" Harlow said hotly. "Listen, Gen, I understand that you're angry about what went down. I am too. But you can't be mad at me for checking on you to make sure that it doesn't happen again. Don't you see how this puts me in a no-win situation? And for the record, if you're sleeping with Shaun, it *is* my business. Cash is my—" She clamped her mouth shut, not sure what to say about Cash. They'd only just decided to try to work things out, and after a year apart, it felt weird to call him her boyfriend again.

"Your what, Harlow?" Imogen asked with her eyes narrowed.

"My person," she finally said. "Shaun is his brother and if you two are involved, then that affects us, too."

"I don't see how," her sister said stubbornly. "What Shaun and I do or don't do really isn't about you or Cash at all. But if you must know, last night wasn't the first time we've been together. I doubt it will be the last. As for labeling our relationship, we just haven't given it one, all right? Is that enough for you? Or do you need to know that this started about two months ago when Shaun came to Napa for a brief vacation?" Imogen pushed her hair out of her eyes and continued. "And before you ask, it's still in the beginning stages, and neither of us knew the other was going to be here. Can't say I'm mad he showed up, though."

"This isn't the first time you've been together?" Harlow asked, her mind reeling.

"No." Imogen let out a humorless chuckle. "What else do you want to know? Exactly how many times we've slept together, or is a rough estimate enough? Maybe where we were when he first kissed me? How about the first time he called, acting like he was worried about you and Cash, but instead he was really checking on me? Or how he'd call every couple of days, and we became friends first, and then things just progressed from there? Do you need a time, date, and location of the first time he felt me up?"

"That's enough," Harlow said coolly. "You know what I meant. I was never looking for intimate details. Only an update on your relationship. Do whatever you want, Gen. I won't bother you again." She turned on her heel and stalked toward the back door. Just as she was leaving, she heard her sister call after her.

"Finally! Now I can get to work on my website. The sooner I get the business up and running, the sooner I'll be on my own where people don't just walk into my bedroom without knocking!"

Harlow ground her teeth together, refusing to engage any further. For the past year, all she'd wanted was to protect her sister. What had she gotten in return? Anger and resentment. Now she was done. She couldn't live her life for someone else and never should have tried.

CHAPTER 16

"So, it looks like things are back on with Harlow," Shaun said as he pulled his truck into a parking space at Hollow Hardware.

"We're going to give it another try." Cash glanced at his brother. "What about you and Imogen? Was that just a one-night thing or..."

Shaun cleared his throat. "It's not a one-night thing."

"Okay. What does that mean?" Cash wasn't sure what to think. Imogen was like a sister to him. On the one hand, he'd like to see his brother happy and dating again, but if he wasn't serious about Imogen, that was going to be nothing but trouble.

"It means exactly what I said." Shaun pushed his door open and jumped out. "Come on. Let's get those supplies before they close so we can get back to work on the house."

Cash met his brother at the front of the truck. "You're really not going to tell me what's going on with you and Imogen?"

Shaun glanced at Cash from the corner of his eye and then shook his head. "Not yet."

"Fair enough," Cash said as they made their way toward the store. "Just be careful with her. I don't want to see her hurt."

Shaun snorted out a humorless laugh. "I don't think it's her you need to worry about."

That statement caught Cash off guard. "You really like her, don't you?"

Shaun shrugged one shoulder.

Cash knew he was trying to be noncommittal, but he saw right through his brother. He cared about Imogen and was worried that whatever they had going on wasn't going to last. Cash clapped his brother on the back and said, "Good luck, man. I know it's never easy, but in my experience, a Thane girl is worth it."

"I'm counting on it," Shaun said, giving him a wry smile.

Once they were in the store, Cash said, "I'm headed to flooring. Do you want to get the paint?"

"Sure."

They parted ways, and Cash cut down the lighting aisle, intending to check out the fixtures for the kitchen before getting the flooring. It was time to replace the flying saucer drop lights over the island bar. But as soon as he rounded the corner, all thoughts of fixture shopping were forgotten when he spotted a woman studying a row of chandeliers. Right behind her was the shadow of a dark spirit and a large box that was teetering on the edge of the shelf above her.

Cash bolted toward the woman, knocking her out of the way just before the box came crashing down on her head. The woman let out a startled cry as the pair fell to the cement floor. A second later, the box crashed to the floor, right where she'd been standing.

The woman let out another startled cry and then turned to Cash, her eyes wide and her hands shaking. "You saved me?"

"Not yet," Cash replied as he hopped back onto his feet and produced his iron chain. The spirit shot straight toward him, its arms raised and its mouth open as it let out a bloodcurdling scream. Cash stepped to the side, whipped out his iron chain, and instantly trapped the spirit, stopping her from whatever further destruction she'd planned to unleash.

"Wh-what is happening?" the woman asked in a shaky voice as she stared in horror at the spirit that had materialized when Cash captured her with his iron chain.

Cash studied the spirit. She looked to have died in her early fifties, had frizzy salt-and-pepper hair, and was glaring at the woman who had just pushed herself to her feet. "Did you know you were being haunted by this ghost?"

"You've been haunting me?" the woman yelled at the spirit. "Are you the reason I've suddenly become so freakin' accident prone this past year? Are you why I've had a broken wrist, a sprained ankle, and a concussion?"

The spirit shot eye daggers at the woman and strained against the iron chain but was unable to free herself.

"Do you know who this spirit is?" Cash asked the woman.

"Oh, yeah. That's my cousin Wendy. After she died, I married her husband. I think she's a tad bit upset about that."

Wendy writhed, and when one arm broke free of the chain, she took a swing at the woman.

"Now, Wendy," she said in an impatient tone. "What was Carl supposed to do? Sit around and be lonely for the rest of his life? I'd thought you'd be happy that he had companionship."

The spirit opened her mouth and let out a silent cry, her energy so strong it was almost too much for Cash to handle.

"Whoa. I think it's best if you stop engaging with her," Cash told the woman. "You're only agitating her, and I'll never be able to banish her when she's this riled up."

The woman crossed her arms over her chest and glared at Wendy. "I can't help it if she's mad that Carl is happier and more satisfied now that he's with me."

Wendy had heard enough. Despite Cash's hold on the iron chain, the spirit gathered enough energy that she disappeared altogether and reappeared seconds later, her hands wrapped around her cousin's neck.

The woman's face turned bright red, and she let out a choking noise.

"Dammit!" Magic rushed through Cash as he raised his arms and called, "By the sun and the moon and the earth and the shadows, please spirit, release the energy that binds Wendy to the present!"

Magic rushed from his fingertips and wrapped around Wendy, zapping the energy that gave her the strength to throttle her cousin. When her fingers slipped from the other woman's neck, Cash once again trapped her with his iron chain. The spirit was completely immobilized this time, but Cash knew he'd never be able to banish her by himself. She was too strong. The best he could do was hold her until help arrived.

"You saved me," the woman choked out, rubbing her neck. "Twice."

"Yeah. Now don't taunt your cousin again, or she may just get a third chance at you." After wrapping the iron chain around his fist, he used the other hand to whip out his phone and call Harlow.

"Hey. I was just thinking about you," Harlow said into the phone, a smile in her voice.

"I'm glad to hear it," he said, unable to keep from grinning.

He liked hearing that he was on her mind. "Are you busy?"

"Not particularly. What's up?"

"Can you come to Hollow Hardware? I've got an insanely jealous ghost who is trying to end her cousin, and she's too strong for me to banish. I could use your help."

There was a long, silent pause before Harlow said, "Do I want to know how you ended up in the middle of this?"

"I was minding my own business in the hardware store when I saw the ghost trying to flatten this lady. I saved her from being crushed by a heavy box, and all hell broke loose from there. I've got the spirit trapped now, but without you, all of this will have been for nothing. She'll be back to tormenting her cousin in no time."

Harlow let out a heavy sigh. "All right. I'll be right there. Where can I find you?"

"Lighting department."

When Cash ended the call, he looked at the woman. "What's your name?"

"Jelly."

"Jelly?" Cash asked, certain he'd heard her wrong.

"Yes, it's a nickname for Jelsa."

Cash nodded. "Hi, Jelly. I'm Cash, and my partner is on her way. Once she gets here, we'll banish your cousin for good so she can no longer attack you."

Jelly frowned. "Banish her to where? Hell?"

"Oh no." Cash shook his head. "To the shadow world. Where they go after that is not up to me to decide."

"Damn," she said with a disappointed sigh. "Wendy was a real B if you know what I mean."

"I think I've got an idea," Cash said with a nod. Leave it to him to end up helping someone with crazy family drama.

His phone buzzed with a text.

It was Shaun. *Where are you?*

Cash texted him back one handed, and a few moments later, Shaun appeared beside him.

"Can't say hanging out with you is boring," Shaun said, shaking his head. "I swear, you can't go anywhere without getting into trouble."

"It's not his fault," Jelly said, gushing as she reached for Cash's arm and held on. "He saved my life." She looked up at Cash and batted her eyelashes. "Does this mean I need to be your servant for seven years? I don't mean to brag, but I did win best homemade pie at the county fair three years in a row." She glanced down at her crotch and then pumped her eyebrows suggestively. "I'd be more than happy to introduce you to my cherry pie."

"Oh wow," Shaun said, shaking his head in disbelief.

Cash suddenly felt some sympathy for Wendy. If he'd had to be subjected to Jelly for any length of time, he might be inclined to throttle her, too. "Thanks for that... ah, generous offer, but I think I'm going to have to pass."

"Your loss," she said with a shrug.

"No doubt," Cash muttered and shared an incredulous look with Shaun.

When Harlow finally arrived, Cash didn't think he'd ever been happier to see another human in his entire life. Jelly had been chattering nonstop about Carl and how she'd always felt like someone was watching them when they did the deed, but now she knew it was Wendy being a dirty peeper.

"Thank the gods," Cash said to Harlow, meeting her troubled eyes. "I tried to banish the spirit with a spell, but her energy was too strong. Can you handle this?"

Harlow glanced at Jelly. "Do you have anything you want to say to this ghost?"

Cash let out the smallest groan. He should have remembered that she'd ask that.

"Actually, I want to tell her that all those years she spent complaining about the size of Carl's—"

"That's enough," Cash said. "There's nothing to fix here. Just a deceased spouse who is mad her cousin married her husband."

"I see," Harlow said with a short nod. She glanced once more at Jelly. "The size of Carl's... uh, *manhood* aside, is there anything important you need to say or ask before I finish this?"

"Well, no, other than to tell her I hope she rots in a Tofu Express for the rest of eternity for trying to kill me," Jelly said and then walked off, not even waiting to see if Harlow was successful.

"A Tofu Express?" Shaun asked. "isn't that a vegan fast-food place?"

"Yes!" Jelly called back as she paused to look over her shoulder. "Wendy always said it'd be a cold day in hell before she ate there. I figured it would be a good resting spot for her."

"No doubt," Shaun said, looking amused.

"Cash, are you ready?" Harlow asked him.

"Yep."

"Good. On the count of three, release the spirit and I'll do my thing."

After Cash nodded, Harlow said, "Three, two, one!"

Cash quickly released the spirit from the confines of his iron chain. The moment Wendy was free, she started screaming like a banshee, making Cash's entire body turn clammy as his stomach roiled.

Harlow, on the other hand, didn't appear to be physically affected by the spirit's wailing and stepped forward in one swift movement and nailed her to one of the wooden shelves. Instantly, the noise stopped and the store was eerily silent.

"That was... a lot," Harlow said as she got into the spirit's face. "This is what you get for trying to kill your cousin."

Wendy opened her mouth, but no words formed. She'd been silenced. Without any emotion at all, Harlow twisted the iron spike, and Wendy shimmered for a moment before the spirit shattered into a million particles of light.

Cash stood there, watching until finally every single bit of light winked out.

Harlow put her spike back in her pocket and turned to Cash. "Was that necessary?"

"Banishing her? Of course it—"

"No," Harlow said, cutting him off. "I mean calling me and forcing me to come down here to deal with that drama. Too bad you didn't film it. It could have been your demo for your new *Real Spirits of Keating Hollow* pilot."

Cash pressed his lips together in a thin line and forced himself to answer in a calm tone, despite the fact that he was majorly offended that she'd just implied he was still looking for a television show. "Funny. What else was I supposed to do? That spirit has been wreaking havoc on her cousin for over a year now. If that box she was nudging off the shelf had hit her target, Jelly would be splattered all over this cement floor."

Shaun snickered, but when both of them turned to glare at him, he clamped his mouth shut and retreated out of the aisle, giving them their privacy.

Cash turned his attention back to Harlow and waited for whatever wrath she was going to unleash on him.

"Can we go outside?" she asked, her voice lowered. "I'd rather not have an audience."

Cash noticed that a couple of other customers were

hovering. He wondered how long they'd been there and then decided it didn't matter. "Yeah, lead the way."

He followed her until they were out on the sidewalk and far enough away from the doors that they wouldn't be putting on a show for anyone.

Harlow stuffed her hands into her jean pockets and lifted her chin as she met his gaze. "I'm not in the ghost hunting business anymore."

"Neither am I," Cash said.

"But that's what you asked me to do today, Cash. Can't you see that? I don't want to be the go-to person that people call when they're being haunted. We've been back together for all of like eight hours, and already you have me out here banishing ghosts for people we don't even know. And frankly, who seem a little insane."

He couldn't argue that last point. "Listen, Harlow, I'm sorry I got you involved in this. But it's not like I went looking for this woman. I rounded the corner and there she was with a ghost trying to attack her. I couldn't just do nothing, could I? You know you wouldn't have walked away if you saw someone in danger."

"Of course not," she said, rubbing her forehead and squinting as if the conversation pained her. "I just don't know why we have to come running. There are mediums who specialize in eradicating spirits, you know."

Cash took a deep breath and let it out slowly. "Yeah, there are. I don't know if there are any here in Keating Hollow, but I guess the next time I see someone in serious danger, I'll recommend they call someone."

"Oh, come on, Cash. I didn't say that." Harlow let out a frustrated sigh. "I'm sorry. It's just that Imogen and I had a fight today, and now I'm dealing with ghosts again. When she finds out, I'm sure I'll be in for another tongue lashing."

"I'm sorry, gorgeous," Cash said, suddenly softening. He opened his arms to her, and when she stepped into them, all the tension drained from his shoulders. It was far too early to be having a disagreement right after their reconciliation.

"I'm sorry, too," she mumbled into his chest. "You did exactly what I would've done. I just hate that no matter where we go, we never seem to get any peace from the spirits."

"We spent too many years inviting them into our energies. We can't just turn that off. It's a part of us now."

She pulled away just enough to look up at him and gave him a wry smile as she said, "Maybe we should really get on that research and figure out how to do a soul cleanse."

He let out a soft chuckle. They'd joked about that many times before. As far as they knew, there wasn't any way to cleanse a soul without causing harm. "Does Keating Hollow have an extensive library?"

"There's a library, but I haven't checked it out yet," she said.

"We'll do that. Soon... when I take you on a date." Cash kissed her temple. "Thank you for helping today. I wouldn't have called except the spirit was homicidal. Next time, as long as the haunted person's life isn't in danger, I'll send them to a currently practicing ghost hunter."

"Thank you," Harlow said and pressed up on her tiptoes to give Cash a kiss. "That's all I can ask for."

"It's not all you could ask," Cash said, his fingers automatically closing over the velvet ring box he always had in his pocket, wishing he could just slip the ring on her finger and ask her to marry him... again. But that would be insane since she'd barely let him back in her life. He needed patience, but it was hard to come by when all he wanted was her in his bed every night and at his breakfast table every morning.

"What should I be asking for, Cash? A candlelight dinner? A walk under the moonlight? Foot massage?"

He chuckled. "I'd be happy to oblige on all of those, but I'm afraid the offer expires at midnight."

She raised one eyebrow. "You know I have plans tonight."

"Surely you're not staying out *all* night with your new friends," he said, keeping his tone light. "You know where I'll be later. I certainly wouldn't mind being woken up by a gorgeous woman climbing in my bed."

Harlow groaned. "Stop tempting me. I have to get some sleep tonight. I have to work tomorrow."

"I bet you'd sleep better after I'm done with you." He'd give just about anything to have her back in his bed that night. He'd missed her more than he'd thought humanly possible. He licked his lips while he let his gaze travel over her body.

"You're not behaving, Cash," Harlow said, sounding a little breathy.

"I know." He dipped his head and pressed soft kisses to her neck just below her ear, in that one spot that always made her shiver. This afternoon was no exception. He felt the small tremor just before she pressed her body to his and moved so that their lips met in a heated kiss.

Cash wanted to put her in the truck and drive her back to his place right that moment. He might have done it if someone hadn't cleared their throat, interrupting them. He took a step back from Harlow and then met his brother's amused gaze. "Shaun, what did you need?"

His brother let out a low chuckle. "Just wanted to let you know that the store is getting ready to close. If you want those wood planks, I think we'd better grab them now."

Dammit. He'd forgotten everything except the woman standing in front of him. "Tonight," he said. "No time is too late." He kissed her one last time before he turned and walked back into the store with his brother on his heels.

"I thought I was going to have to turn a firehose on you two," Shaun said as they filled a cart with wood flooring.

Cash glanced up at him. "Fair warning. Harlow's coming over later tonight. If you haven't gotten those noise-canceling headphones yet, I suggest you find somewhere else to be."

Shaun's lips curved up into a hint of a smile. "That I can do."

CHAPTER 17

*H*arlow felt like she needed a shower after banishing the spirit of Jelly's cousin. In all of her years dealing with ghosts, that may have been the most ridiculous situation she'd encountered. Usually the spirits that didn't move on were in the present because they had unfinished business. That certainly seemed to be the case for Wendy, too, but usually it didn't involve trying to murder a close relative. Did Carl have a magic schlong or something? The thought made Harlow grimace, and she did her best to put the entire encounter out of her mind.

She walked into the house and found Imogen at a small desk in the dining room area. "Hey, that's new."

"Yeah. I got it off Marketplace for a steal." Imogen turned to look at Harlow. "Where have you been?"

Dread coiled in Harlow's gut as she braced herself for backlash. Imogen had been out running errands and apparently picking up the desk when Cash had called earlier. "Cash called with a ghost emergency. He needed help banishing a spirit."

Imogen's jaw tightened, but instead of the backlash Harlow expected, she just asked, "Is this going to be a normal thing now that you and Cash are an item again?"

"No. This was just a one-off. A woman was in danger. He couldn't just walk away."

Her sister nodded once and then turned back to her computer. That was unexpected. Not wanting to rock the boat, Harlow moved into the kitchen for some water and asked, "Are you still working on your website?"

"I did as much as I could with that, and now I'm working on a design for my business cards."

"Business cards. Wow. Moving fast."

Letting out a sigh, Imogen turned to her. "What's that supposed to mean?"

"Whoa." Harlow raised her hands in the air. "I didn't mean anything. I'm just impressed, that's all." So much for burying the hatchet. It looked like they'd still be walking on eggshells for a while.

Imogen closed her eyes and muttered something to herself that Harlow couldn't hear.

"Sorry," Harlow snapped. Then she tried her best to keep her voice neutral as she continued. "I'm going to go get cleaned up. If you're still up for girls' night, we need to leave in an hour."

Imogen didn't say anything.

Harlow ground her teeth together and wondered if there would ever be a time when she and Imogen didn't have a wall of tension between them. Resigned that there was no way to fix it, she retreated to the back of the house and took that shower she'd been craving.

～

When Harlow walked into the living room an hour later, Imogen was standing near the door, a jacket folded over her arm, and Harlow gave her sister a genuine smile. "I'm glad to see you're still venturing out tonight."

"It's better than staying in, right?" Imogen asked.

"Definitely," Harlow agreed and then led the way outside to her Subaru. Neither of them said a word all the way to town. Unable to take the silence, Harlow turned on the radio and hummed along with the latest Silver Scars hit, the band that featured Levi Kelley. When she glanced at her sister, she saw her mouthing the words, too. At least they had common ground somewhere.

When the song ended, Imogen said, "I really like that song."

"Me, too. I'm hoping we can get Levi to play at Equinox one day when he's back in town."

Imogen's eyes lit up. "That would be amazing."

They continued to talk music right up until they walked into Incantation Café, and Harlow was grateful for the temporary truce.

"Harlow, you made it!" Hanna said the moment they stepped through the door. "And this must be your sister."

Harlow smiled at the gorgeous woman and nodded. "Hanna, this is my sister Imogen."

"It's really nice to meet you," Imogen said, shaking Hanna's hand.

"We're very happy to have you along. With you here, it makes it even teams," she said with a giggle.

"Teams?" Imogen asked with her eyebrows raised in alarm. "No one said anything about a competition."

Hanna laughed. "It's nothing serious. Just a friendly golf cart race down by the river. Winners get bragging rights."

"You need teams for golf cart races?" Imogen asked curiously.

"Sure. Someone needs to cast spells while the driver handles the golf cart." Hanna's phone rang and she put up a finger. "Give me a second."

While Hanna answered the call, Imogen turned to Harlow. "Spells?"

"Don't ask me. This is the first I'm hearing about any of this."

Imogen looked like a deer in the headlights. "I feel like I should have brushed up on my magic skills a little more. I can't imagine what kind of a spell someone might need for a golf cart race."

Harlow had no idea either, but she wasn't worried. Hanna and the rest of them were good people. Whatever it was, Harlow was just grateful she and Imogen had been included. It was the perfect way to ease back into some fun quality time with her sister.

"Good news!" Hanna said after she ended the call. "Wanda and Abby will be here any moment. Let's head out so I can lock up and they won't have to wait for us."

Once outside, Harlow heard music first, and when she turned, she spotted two golf carts headed straight for them, both of them complete spectacles. One was glittery purple with flashing strobe lights. Prince's "1999" blared from the speakers as Wanda, the driver, sang the lyrics at the top of her lungs.

Right behind her, Abby drove an orange golf cart that was covered in twinkle lights and had daisy decals and long eyelashes on the headlights. She was also singing along with the lyrics, but she was being drowned out by Wanda.

"Wow," Imogen said. "They take this golf cart thing seriously, don't they?"

"You have no idea," Hanna said with a laugh.

Harlow grinned, loving it. This night out with the girls was exactly what she needed. Wanda and Abby parked their carts right in front of the café, and before they could even hop out, Yvette Townsend-Burton, Brinn Taylor, and Miranda Moon walked up, chattering about Miranda's latest book signing they'd had at Hollow Books, the bookstore that Yvette and her husband, Jacob, owned.

Harlow waved and gave them a smile.

Miranda grinned when she saw her. "It's good to see you out, Harlow."

Hanna, who hadn't seen them yet, spun around. "You're here!" She gave each one a quick hug and then waved at Imogen. "You have to meet Harlow's sister, Imogen." After she introduced everyone and Imogen looked more than a little overwhelmed by their enthusiastic welcome, Hanna clapped her hands together. "Come on. Let's get out of here. I'm ready for some fun."

"Did someone say fun?" Wanda asked, opening a cooler on the back of her cart. "Anyone ready for a beer, cider, or wine? I've got plenty."

Harlow walked over and glanced inside. "You really are prepared."

"Always," Wanda said with a wink. "What can I get you?"

"I'll try a Keating Hollow cider."

"Me, too," Imogen said.

Harlow nearly jumped right out of her skin. She hadn't realized her sister was standing right behind her.

"Two ciders coming right up." Wanda grabbed the bottles,

twisted the caps off, and then tucked them into bottle koozies. "Here you go. Anyone else?"

The other four each got something alcoholic, but the two designated drivers opted for water.

"Okay, pick a golf cart," Hanna said, already climbing into the orange cart next to Abby.

Yvette slid into the seat next to Wanda.

And while Imogen and Harlow stood frozen, not sure what to do, Brinn got in Abby's cart and Miranda took a seat in Wanda's.

"I guess we'd better pick one," Harlow told her sister.

Imogen nodded and slid into the back seat of Abby's cart next to Brinn.

Harlow took a seat next to Miranda. "I guess you're stuck with me."

"And thank the goddess for that," the author said, holding up her drink for a toast. "I can't think of a better partner in crime."

Harlow chuckled, tapped her bottle to Miranda's, and then took a long swig of the delicious pear cider that she'd heard was made by Rhys Silver, Hanna's husband. He specialized in ciders at the Keating Hollow Brewery.

The two golf carts sped down Main Street and then veered off onto a pathway that led down to the river. The almost full moon shimmered off the calm water. With the mountains illuminated in the background, it was so gorgeous it almost didn't look real. Not for the first time, Harlow found herself thanking the universe that she'd found the magical town. She couldn't imagine living anywhere else now.

"Okay," Wanda said, killing the music and jumping out of her golf cart. "Since we have newbies, we need to go over the rules."

"There aren't any rules," Abby called as she got off her cart.

Wanda placed her hands on her hips and *tsked* as she shook her head. "There *are* a few rules, Abby. You just like to pretend otherwise."

Everyone chuckled at the mock outrage on Abby's face.

Wanda gestured to Harlow and Imogen. "The plan is to have this golf cart race and then hang out for however long anyone wants to. If anyone is hungry after, we're headed for pizza."

"Cool," Harlow said. "I'm good for whatever."

"Me, too," Imogen said, but she kept tugging at a lock of her hair, a sure sign that she was nervous.

Wanda noticed and reached over, squeezing her hand.

Imogen's expression cleared, and Harlow wondered if Wanda had some sort of calming magic. If she did, it would explain why she was such a successful realtor.

"Okay, rules," Wanda said, sounding more serious than ever. "One of us will cast a spell for a countdown clock, and when it hits zero, we take off. The rules are that there are no rules except each golf cart has to make it around that tree down there before heading back, and then whoever passes this starting point first wins."

Imogen cleared her throat. "What does that mean, no rules?"

"It means we can cast any type of spell we want to slow down the other golf cart," Brinn said. "Within reason of course. No curses or anything sinister like that."

"See, we do have rules," Wanda said, giving Abby a look of superiority.

"Pardon me. It never occurred to me that one of our friends might curse someone," Abby said with an eyeroll. "But you're right. We do have some rules."

"Ah-ha!" Wanda said. "You heard her. She said I'm right, and you all are my witnesses."

Everyone chuckled and shook their heads as Wanda and Abby continued to hurl harmless barbs at each other.

"Um, okay, so what do the winners get?" Imogen asked.

"Bragging rights!" Wanda and Abby said at the same time and then both dissolved into laughter.

"They used to make actual bets on these races," Yvette explained. "But when the stakes got to be too ridiculous, Drew put his foot down. That's Abby and Yvette's brother-in-law, who also happens to be the town sheriff. Their last bet involved some minor graffiti that didn't go over well."

Harlow raised her eyebrows. What had she gotten herself and Imogen into? She didn't mind bending a rule every now and then if circumstances warranted it, but otherwise, she was a rule follower... at least when it came to the law. "Graffiti? Where?"

Abby rolled her eyes. "It wasn't that terrible, and I used washable paint. It all came off in the next big rain."

"What did you paint?" Imogen asked, looking amused.

"The sidewalks of Main Street. I lost, so I had to write *Wanda is the queen of the world*. Then I painted her face with a crown on her head. It wasn't great, but it got the point across."

"Some people still call me Queen Wanda," Wanda said, blowing on her nails and then pretending to buff them on her shirt. "It was glorious."

"A few business owners complained," Abby said, rolling her eyes. "And Drew had to hear all about it. He was not thrilled to say the least."

"That's because it didn't rain for a hundred and forty-two days afterward, and we were in drought conditions so we couldn't just use a water hose to wash it off," Wanda said with a hearty laugh. Then she sobered. "Drew was ready to throttle us. He made us promise no more bets on the golf cart races. It hasn't been the same since."

"Please," Abby said. "You're still Queen Wanda. And if you recall, the last time I lost, I made you your favorite shortbread cookies."

Wanda brightened. "Oh, yeah. Well that didn't suck. I love lemon shortbread."

"Oh, I adore lemon shortbread," Imogen piped in.

"You're my kind of girl," Wanda said and then turned to Abby. "Loser has to bake the winner cookies. Baker's choice?"

"You're on!" Abby shook her hand and then climbed back into her golf cart.

CHAPTER 18

*H*arlow's body hummed with excited nervous energy. How long had it been since she'd done anything as fun as a silly golf cart race? She honestly didn't know, but it was much longer than her year of exile from Cash and ghost hunting. Even before that, she'd been so focused on her career that her idea of fun had been researching historically haunted locations and then deciding whether it was worth checking them out.

A chill washed over her, and she wrapped her arms around her body, trying to stave off the gooseflesh. Her life had solely revolved around her career and Cash. Even Imogen had been just a side character in her life. She wondered, if she'd been closer to her sister, if she'd have noticed sooner that something had been terribly off about her behavior before the spirit had managed to go through all of her resources. The guilt that had been eating away at her for months intensified.

The answer was staring her in the face.

Yes.

"Hanna? Can you set the countdown clock?" Wanda called, pulling Harlow out of her sudden maudlin thoughts.

Harlow shook her head, silently scolding herself for not staying in the moment. She was done worrying about the past. At least for the moment. Tonight was about connecting with the women of Keating Hollow and finally letting her hair down.

"On it!" Hanna called. The witch stepped out of the golf cart and raised her arms in the air. Magic suddenly crackled at her fingertips. With a determined look on her pretty face, she pointed at the river and called, "Goddess of the waters, help us set a clock. Count us down from three, so we can fly like bees."

Everyone laughed at her silly spell. And when nothing happened, Wanda said, "Looks like the goddess isn't super impressed with your spell work, Hanna."

Hanna frowned. "I don't know why that didn't work." She scrunched up her face in concentration and repeated the incantation, only this time she touched the pentacle pendant she wore around her neck with one hand and added, "So mote it be."

Instantly, magic shot from her fingertips toward the water, and a spout of water shot up and hurtled toward the golf carts, already forming what looked like a digital clock with the number 3 in it.

It was an impressive bit of magic to be able to manipulate water like that. No wonder she'd needed the help of her pentacle. For trickier spells, it helped to harness the magic through a talisman.

"Remember! No rules!" Wanda called as the numbers counted down to one.

Both golf carts took off, speeding along the river as the women all let out cries of excitement. Immediately Hanna cast a spell, sending a cloud of rain over Wanda's cart. The water rushed down, causing Wanda to curse under her breath when the visibility was reduced to nearly zero. She turned the windshield wipers on, but they were no match for the rain.

"I've got this!" Yvette called and sent a ball of fire right at the raincloud. It burst, and the rain dissipated.

Harlow was in awe as she watched Yvette, Brinn, Hanna, and Miranda fire off randomly harmless spells that would slow each of the golf carts down. There was everything from fog to lightning bugs and potholes to speed bumps.

"Show us what you've got, Harlow!" Wanda called over her shoulder. Harlow bit down on her bottom lip and racked her brain, trying to think of something. While she was a witch, her talent was in communicating with and banishing ghosts. She sure as heck wasn't going to summon one. That was the last thing she'd do. But the thought of spirits gave her an idea. They often times showed up as light before they materialized. And when that happened, she could sometimes ward them off with a bolt of her own shimmering magic. She closed her eyes and imagined a celebration of sparkling light encircling Abby's cart and then called, "Illuminate!"

Magic materialized and formed a ribbon of magical light that whipped around the other golf cart in a tornado fashion, causing them to come to a stop.

Wanda let out a whoop as she rounded a tree and passed the stopped golf cart.

It took the other team a few seconds to break Harlow's spell, and Wanda put her fist in the air, already celebrating.

But a few yards before the finish line, colorful animated gnomes appeared and started dancing around Wanda's golf cart. She swerved, doing her best not to hit any, but it slowed them way down.

Harlow blinked, taken completely off guard. Then she let out a loud laugh when she realized the spell had been cast by Imogen. She leaned forward and said, "Wanda, they aren't real. Drive right through them. They're an illusion."

"Seriously?" Wanda glanced back over her shoulder, and when Harlow nodded, she tightened her grip on the steering wheel and powered on. But it was too late.

Abby's golf cart shot forward, and the other team won the race by less than a foot.

The other team jumped out of their cart and started dancing around in celebration. Wanda and Yvette joined them, but Harlow sat in the back of Wanda's golf cart, feeling uneasy. The air had suddenly gotten sticky, and the hair on her arms was standing up.

That meant one thing.

A ghost.

She held her breath, praying it wasn't Crazy Cora. Without any thought, she automatically reached for her iron spike. Then she forced herself to leave it in place. If it was Cora, the spike wasn't going to help. There was no need to brandish it and worry her sister. At least if it was a crazy ghost, she had an entire circle of witches who could help if needed.

"Can you see her?" Brinn asked.

Harlow startled, having not even realized that Brinn was still sitting next to her. "See who?"

"The spirit. You feel her, don't you?"

"Yes. Do you?" Harlow asked.

"I saw her first." Hanna gestured to the river, where an ethereal spirit was walking along the far bank with her face tilted toward the moon. "Then I felt you stiffen. Don't worry, she's harmless. All she ever does is wander under the moonlight."

Harlow stared at the spirit in curiosity. "Do you know who she is?"

"Sure. That's Willa Keating. She's one of the town's founders," Brinn said.

"And she just roams the river?" Harlow asked. "Never goes anywhere else?"

"Not that I'm aware of. I've never seen her anywhere else."

Harlow nodded. "I see." Then she tore her gaze from the spirit. "You're a medium, too?"

She gave Harlow a whisper of a smile and nodded. "I obviously knew you were. My husband and I used to watch your show all the time before you decided to step away. Can't say I blame you. Dealing with hostile spirits is draining in the extreme."

Harlow felt an instant connection with Brinn. It wasn't often that she met another medium who didn't want to pick her brain or talk endlessly about her show. All of them seemed to want their own show, and most wanted Harlow to help them get it. Brinn wasn't giving off any of that kind of energy.

"I wonder what made her appear," Brinn said, staring at Willa.

"Is it unusual for her to appear?"

"Yes. Usually only on the solstice or when the veil is thin to the spirit world."

Harlow felt a wave of unease wash over her, and she wondered if *she* was the reason the spirit had appeared.

Just as she had the thought, Imogen let out a loud laugh, and the spirit turned in her direction.

Harlow stared, wondering why the spirit was focused on her sister. Was she drawn to her? And if so, why? As Imogen's laughter died down, the spirit slowly started to fade into the ether. Harlow blinked and Willa was gone. She glanced at the last place she saw the spirit and then to her sister.

Imogen was chatting with the ladies of Keating Hollow, getting information for her wedding planning business. There wasn't anything out of the ordinary. But still, Harlow couldn't help feeling like she was missing something. She just didn't know what.

"Harlow, Brinn, get over here," Wanda called. "Abby brought chocolate."

"Can't resist that," Brinn said as she climbed out of the golf cart. "Are you coming?"

Harlow nodded. "Definitely.

A couple hours later, as Harlow and Imogen waved to Wanda when she dropped them off in front of the Incantation Café, Harlow's heart felt full. She'd gotten to know a few of the ladies of Keating Hollow, but this was the first time she'd really felt like she was part of the community and not just the bartender who kept the drinks coming.

Harlow hit the key fob to unlock the doors of her Subaru and then took her place behind the wheel. Imogen follow suit and was smiling to herself as she settled into the passenger seat.

"Did you have a good time?" Harlow asked as she backed out of the parking space.

"Yeah. Who knew golf cart races were so brutal?"

They both laughed.

"Nice one with the gnomes. I had no idea that spell was going to come in handy so quickly," Harlow said as she pulled out onto the two-lane road that headed back to their house.

"Right?" Imogen said with a smile. "Hanna said breakfast is on her the next time I'm at the café. Which, coincidentally, is going to be tomorrow because she said I can pick her brain about wedding vendors."

Harlow returned her smile. "That's really nice of her."

"I thought so, too." Imogen let out a contented sigh. "You know what, Harlow?"

"What's that, Gen?"

"I think getting laid off and being forced to move to Keating Hollow may have been the best thing that could've happened. Thanks for the bedroom and for hooking me up with your friends. I really appreciate it."

Harlow had to swallow the lump in her throat as emotion threatened to overwhelm her. It had been so long since she'd seen her sister happy, much less happy with anything that Harlow had done. She'd almost forgotten what this easiness between them had felt like. She reached over and squeezed her sister's hand briefly and, in a slightly gruff voice, said, "You're welcome."

CHAPTER 19

"I hope that's you, Harlow. Otherwise, Shaun's about to get an eyeful," Cash said as he heard footsteps on the other side of the bathroom door.

"You do know that robes exist, right?" Shaun said, sounding impatient.

"What fun would that be when I can horrify my brother with my naked ass?" he asked just to get a rise out of him as he wrapped a towel around his torso and tied it low on his hips. After the spirit incident at Hollow Hardware, they'd come back to the house and spent several hours working on the flooring. Then when he got a text that Harlow was on her way, he'd hopped in the shower.

Shaun groaned. "You're never going to let me live that down, are you?"

"Nope." Cash used a towel to dry his hair as he asked, "What do you want?"

"I need to talk to you. Can you cover your junk and come out here for a minute?"

Cash frowned and pulled the door open. "What's wrong?"

"Nothing, I…" Shaun blew out a breath and ran a hand through his hair, looking a little bewildered.

"Spit it out, whatever it is."

Shaun nodded. "Yeah, okay. I had another vision, but it doesn't make much sense to me. Not unless you're getting ready to cook an elaborate meal and then set up a picnic in the dining room."

Cash's eyebrows rose nearly to his hairline. "No. I'm not even sure if Harlow has eaten yet. I was going to ask her if she's hungry and then order something to be delivered. Like pizza."

Shaun shook his head. "I don't think that's what's in store for you tonight, brother. But if the romantic candlelight picnic doesn't happen, will you let me know?"

"Sure." Cash finally took a good look at his brother. He was already cleaned up and dressed in jeans and a Henley shirt. He wasn't wearing anything special, but he'd shaved, and Cash caught a hint of his subtle aftershave. "Are you headed to spend the evening with Imogen?"

"I can't stay here. Not with Harlow coming over." He winked and then waved as he took off down the stairs. "Have fun. Try to remember that I live here before you start cooking breakfast nude tomorrow morning. I'll be back early. I have to get some work done."

"Breakfast in the nude?" Cash yelled back at him. "Since when is that a thing?"

"Since you're determined to make sure I get a look at your ass," he called up from the bottom of the stairs. A moment later, the front door slammed shut.

Cash shook his head and retreated back to the bathroom for his own shave.

CASH HEARD the crunch of tires on gravel and smiled to himself. Finally. It had only been a handful of hours since he'd seen Harlow, but after their year-long drought, he was desperate just to be near her. With two glasses of wine in hand, he walked out onto the front porch to greet her.

Harlow glanced up at him and gave him that slow, contented smile he's missed so much. The one that said she was exactly where she wanted to be with the person who made her the most comfortable.

"How was girls' night?" Cash asked as Harlow walked up the short flight of stairs.

"Really good." She reached for one of the glasses as she leaned in and gave him a warm kiss.

Cash snaked one arm around her back, pulling her in close. "Can't tell you how much I missed this."

"Kisses?" she asked, smiling up at him.

"Yes, that and you coming home to me after a long day."

Sadness and regret flashed in her dark gaze but were quickly replaced with contentment as she took a sip of her favorite wine. "I missed that, too."

Cash slipped his hand into hers and led her into the house. "Have you eaten dinner?"

"Nope. I was hoping my boyfriend would have something whipped up for me." She gave him a cheeky grin.

He laughed. "Have you forgotten who you're dating?"

"Nope." She took another sip of wine and then kissed his cheek. "That may have just been wishful thinking." Harlow wrinkled her nose. "Got anything in that kitchen of yours we can cook that's edible?"

"Possibly, but how do you feel about pizza?"

"Love it," Harlow said. "But unless you already have one here, we're not getting it tonight."

"What? Why not?" Cash looked at his watch. It was just before nine. "Surely someone is still open."

Harlow laughed and shook her head. "What have you been doing since you showed up in town? They roll the sidewalks up at six, and Mystyk Pizza closes in about five minutes." She shrugged, and this time she was the one to grab his hand and start leading him toward his kitchen. "Come on. Let's see what hasn't started rotting in your fridge. It was looking a little sad last night."

"This could be embarrassing," Cash admitted.

But before they made it even a few feet, soft piano music started playing from the back of the house.

Harlow paused. "Is Shaun here?"

"No," Cash said, his heart sinking as he wondered what Aunt Jane was up to now. "He left about ten minutes before you arrived. Let me just go see what's up."

"Not without me," Harlow said, following him down the hallway. She'd put her wine down and was clutching his hand with both of hers.

Cash could feel a heavy layer of nervous energy radiating from her touch, and it shocked him. In all the years they'd known each other, he'd never known her to be this nervous over anything. He squeezed her hand and said, "I'm sure it's nothing."

"It's not nothing, Cash. And we both know it," she said, slowing her pace as the music grew louder.

"It's probably just Aunt Jane," he said, trying to reassure her.

"Like that makes it any better. The last time she showed up, she gave you a concussion."

Cash didn't have a response for that. It was true. He just

hoped that since he and Harlow were back together that there wouldn't be any more attacks.

When he poked his head into the formal dining room, Cash blinked, trying to take in the scene. He'd cleared out the furniture not long after he'd moved in, intending to refurbish it. But since he hadn't gotten around to that yet, he'd left the room empty and just ate his meals at the kitchen table. Now someone had placed a blanket in the middle of the room, filled it with candles, and set out two covered plates along with what looked like some sort of gourmet salads.

"Oh my gosh, Cash!" Harlow asked in a hushed tone, "Did you do this?"

"No, but I wish I had," he said with awe in his voice. When Shaun told him he'd had this vision, he hadn't truly believed it would come true. If he hadn't checked the house before Shaun left, Cash would have bet money that his brother had set this all up. But he hadn't, and the only answer was that a spirit had done it. "Aunt Jane?" he called. "Is this your handiwork?"

A shimmer on the other side of the room caught his attention. Aunt Jane appeared, smiling mischievously and waving her fingers at them before she started to fade as she slipped through one of the walls, leaving them alone for their romantic dinner date.

"What in the world?" Harlow asked, turning to him with disbelief written all over her face. "How did a ghost put this together?"

"That's a very good question and one I don't have any answers for." Cash tucked her hand into the crook of his arm and led her over to the blanket picnic. "But as long as she went through all of this trouble, we might as well enjoy it."

Harlow let out a bark of laughter as she shook her head. "I just can't believe that this is happening right now."

"You have to give her credit for stepping up her matchmaking game," Cash said as they both lowered themselves to the blanket. "It's a major improvement, don't you think?"

"No doubt about that." Harlow looked down at her covered plate. "I'm a little scared to see what it is."

"I always heard that Aunt Jane was a fabulous cook, so if she made it, it's probably delicious."

"I've never seen a spirit cook before." Harlow placed both hands on the metal cover and then pulled it away as if she were ripping a bandage off. "Oh my gosh. It smells wonderful."

Cash removed his own cover and was treated to a wonderful aroma of garlic and some kind of spices he couldn't identify.

"Risotto. With salmon." Harlow picked up her fork and broke off a piece of salmon before she said, "Oh man, if this is as good as it looks and smells, I think we're gonna have to figure out how to get your aunt to be our personal chef."

Our chef. The implication of what Harlow had just said wasn't lost on Cash. In her mind, she already saw them living together again. "Pretty sure Aunt Jane isn't ever leaving this house, so if you want to employ her for that job, then we're going to have to live here."

Harlow put her fork down without taking a bite and frowned. "Cash, I just signed a two-year lease."

"So?" He held her gaze, trying to decide whether she was really worried about breaking a lease or if she just wasn't ready to think about them living together again. But she was the one who'd implied it first. "You could break it or let Imogen take it over. I'm not seeing that as an insurmountable problem. Do you?"

"No, not really," she chuckled nervously and waved an

unconcerned hand. "I guess I hadn't thought this all the way through, and suddenly I realized I'd locked myself into a long-term contract. And, I don't know, I panicked a little. But you're right. There are solutions. Just need to figure out the right one when the time is right."

He reached across his plate and took her hand gently in his. While caressing the back of her hand with his thumb, he said, "I'm not rushing this. All I care about is spending time with you. But I'll be honest, if you wanted to move in here, I'd help you pack your bags tonight."

Her facial expression was so soft, so full of emotion, that he thought his heart might explode right out of his chest. "I'm not quite there yet, but..." She gave him a shy smile that made his heart skip a beat. "This last year was miserable, and now that you're back in my life, I don't ever want that to change."

Cash fingered the velvet box that was in his pocket. His subconscious screamed for him to pull it out, to put that ring back on her finger, but they hadn't even been a couple for twenty-four hours. Even if his heart was ready to jump back in with both feet, his head told him they still had things to work out. Besides, he wasn't going to ask her to marry him again until he was absolutely certain it was going to mean forever, no matter what. "Can I ask you something?"

She sucked in a breath as if bracing herself for whatever he was going to say. Then she cleared her throat. "Always."

He scooted to sit next to her and put his arm around her shoulders, pulling her into him so that her head was resting on his chest. "Don't be nervous, gorgeous. It's not a pop quiz or anything like that," he teased.

"Stop," she said playfully. "It's been an emotional few days."

"It has," he agreed and kissed her temple. "I just want to

know what you see for your future." He wanted to ask about *their* future but didn't want to put that pressure on her.

"Mine? Not ours?" she asked, looking up at him.

He couldn't help the snort of laughter. "I was going to say that but figured I should start with what *you* wanted first."

"Smart man." She snuggled into his chest again and said, "Well, as far as the immediate future goes, I want to work at Equinox and continue to rebuild my relationships with you and Imogen." She covered his hand with hers. "You and my sister are the most important people in my life. I like having you both here in Keating Hollow where I can see you every day."

"I definitely like being included in your immediate plans," Cash said.

"I bet you do." She chuckled softly.

Cash's insides warmed, and he wondered if she'd mind if he took her to bed before they even finished their dinner.

But then Harlow started talking again and he put the thought out of his mind. He really wanted to know what she was thinking since it was obviously vastly different from when they were television stars.

She turned her head and held his gaze as she said, "I really just want a quiet life here in Keating Hollow, hopefully one with you where we aren't fighting ghosts all the time, or any of the time for that matter. I like working at Equinox because it keeps me busy and makes me feel like part of the community. Other than that, I'm thinking of taking up pottery. Or I would if there was a pottery studio."

He chuckled. "You know if you start pottery you'll never hear the end of that scene in *Ghost*, right? People will be asking you about that all the time."

She cringed. "They would, wouldn't they? Well, it's a risk I'll just have to take. It's something I've always wanted to do. Maybe there's a class over at the coast." She eyed him. "What about you, Cash? What do you want for the future?"

"You." He winked at her.

Harlow thumped him lightly on the chest. "Come on, Cash. Give me more than that."

"It's true though." Running his hand up and down her arm, he added, "Okay, long-term? The one thing I'm sure about is you. As for what I'll do now that we're retired television personalities, I really like what I'm doing here with the house. Maybe I'll get into renovations. Or maybe even build houses here in Keating Hollow. I know the real estate market is tight here. There are plenty of people looking for builders. If I could find subcontractors, it could be really interesting work."

Harlow stared at him for a long moment. Then she raised an eyebrow. "Reality home improvement?"

"Huh?" he asked, taken off guard. Then he frowned at her. "You're asking if I chose that because it could get me back on television?"

"The possibility did cross my mind," she said, sounding slightly guilty for asking.

"Nope. That has nothing to do with it, Harlow. Did you think I missed television that much?" He couldn't believe that her mind had gone there immediately. Since when had he ever been a celebrity chaser?

"Well, yes. No. I don't know." She sat up. "You were so upset when we lost our show. I just thought…" She shook her head. "I know it was important to you."

"Harlow," he said, tilting her head up so that he could hold her gaze. "It wasn't the television that was important to me. It was working together and being with you every day. You must've known that."

She didn't say anything as she let that sink in. Of course she'd known she was important to him, but he'd always been so proud of that show. And he had been upset when they'd lost it. But it seemed she'd misread exactly why. Suddenly, she wrapped her arms around his neck and kissed him. Hard.

His mind jumbled as sensation took over. He was desperate for her touch, to show her just how much he loved and missed her. Talking was good. He knew that, but right then, he just needed to *feel*.

Minutes ticked by as they made out, ignoring the food. Cash was only hungry for the woman who had come willingly to his arms. She was his home. He'd always known that. It didn't really matter what career he chose next or if he even chose one at all. If he had her, it was enough.

Finally, when Harlow broke free, her chest was heaving and her cheeks were flushed with desire.

Cash glanced down at the food. "Are you sure you want to eat now, or can I take you to bed?"

She didn't even bother looking at the full plates. She just said, "To bed."

Cash got to his feet, swept Harlow up in his arms, and carried her to what would someday soon be *their* room.

CHAPTER 20

*H*arlow was luxuriating in Cash's bed the next morning when a series of texts started to chime on her phone.

Cash groaned and rolled over, wrapping his arms around her as he planted kisses along the back of her neck. His voice was full of grit when he muttered, "Ignore it."

Gods, how she wished she could. Their night together had been incredible, and she'd like nothing better than to stay in their love bubble. But just as the sun was pulling them into the new day, so were her responsibilities. "Can't, big guy. It's Imogen." Ever since the possession, Harlow had made it a strict rule that she always answered her sister, no matter the circumstances.

"But it's so early," Cash complained. He tightened his hold on her and pressed his hard body against her, nearly making her forget about everything except the hot-blooded man lying behind her.

When the phone started playing "Grounded" by Silver Scars, Harlow was immediately jolted out of her lust haze.

Pulling out of Cash's embrace, she reached for the phone and said, "Imogen? What's wrong?"

"Good morning, sister," Imogen said cheerfully. "Nothing's wrong. I just have a huge favor to ask."

Harlow sat up and rubbed at her eyes. Then she squinted at the clock on Cash's side of the bed. "Right now? It's practically the crack of dawn."

"Please. I've been up since five, preparing for my day."

"Preparing for what?" Harlow rubbed at her eyes and suppressed a groan.

"I have my first client today," her sister said, pride radiating in her tone.

"What? How?" The news had jolted Harlow awake. Imogen hadn't even done any advertising yet. As far as Harlow knew, all she'd done was start her website, order business cards, and written a simple business plan. "Or more importantly, who is your client?"

"Sadie Lewis. She works at Keating Hollow Brewery, and apparently Abby stopped by there last night on her way home from girls' night. They got to talking, and it turns out that Sadie's cousin is coming to town to get married in a few months and has asked Sadie to put it together for her. Abby passed my name on, and Sadie emailed me right away. We chatted last night and are meeting at the Pelsh winery today at ten."

"Wow. Congratulations!" Harlow was thrilled for her sister and this opportunity. "This is huge. Sadie's been working at the brewery forever. She knows everyone in town. With her as a solid reference, your business should be booming in no time."

"From your lips to the goddess's ears," Imogen said.

"Okay, so what's the favor you need from me?"

Imogen cleared her throat. And when she spoke, her voice was shaky with nervous energy. "Will you come with me?"

"Me? Why?" Harlow asked, completely taken off guard. "I don't know anything about planning weddings. That's your specialty."

"I've got the wedding part covered. I think I just need some moral support. Someone to make sure I don't mess up the business end of it. Will you come?"

Harlow found herself nodding as her entire body lit with joy. She'd missed them relying on each other when big things were happening. "Of course I'll come. Let me get up and get some coffee in me, and then I'll meet you at home and we can go together."

"Okay. That's good." She blew out a breath. "I wanted to get there a little early to tour the place first before Sadie gets there. Do you think you can get here by about a quarter to nine?"

"Can do. See you soon, sis." Harlow ended the call and looked down at Cash. "My sister called."

"I caught that." He reached up, brushed a lock of hair over her shoulder, and then trailed his fingers over her collar bone, his touch sending a shiver of desire through her. "I guess that ruins the plans I had for you this morning."

Harlow covered his hand with hers, stopping his seductive touch. "How about a new plan?"

"What's that," he asked, his sleepy eyes and stubbled jaw making him nearly irresistible.

"Join me in the shower?" She slipped from the bed, not bothering to cover her naked body.

Cash was out of the bed so fast it startled her. Then she let out a bark of laughter as she led him into the bathroom.

Five minutes later, with the hot stream of water sluicing

over them and his hands covering every inch of her body, all of her amusement had vanished.

"This plan is so much better," he murmured against her skin.

Harlow arched her neck back, giving him more access as she murmured her agreement. "*So* much better."

Then the rest of the world slipped away as they got lost in each other one more time before they started their days.

"THERE YOU ARE," Imogen said, pacing the front porch of their rental. Her hair was styled in a sleek ponytail, and she looked chic in her cigarette pants and a flowy white blouse that showed off one shoulder.

"You look great," Harlow said as she glanced at the time on her phone. It was 8:41 am. "Am I late?"

Imogen shrugged. "No. I don't think so. I'm just excited, I guess."

Harlow gestured back to the driveway. "Where's the Mustang?"

"Oh, that." Imogen scowled. "We were going to run out for some things at the grocery store last night, but it started making a squealing noise. We dropped it off at the shop on the way to the store and then Shaun brought me back here. They said it's a belt. Should be fixed sometime today."

Harlow nodded and wondered if that was the real reason that her sister wanted her to go with her to the winery. She needed a ride. The thought depressed her, so she put it out of her head and ran up the stairs. "Let me just drop off my bag and we can get going."

"Yeah, okay. I'll meet you in the car."

"Dang, you are in a rush." Harlow laughed, ran inside, dropped off her bag, and wished she had time for one more cup of coffee before they took off for the winery. Her shower with Cash had severely limited her time before she'd had to rush back home. And after being up half the night, she was already feeling the effects from her lack of sleep the past two nights.

Instead of coffee, she opted for sugar, grabbing a bottle of water and the last two pastries that were on the counter. It would have to do.

Once she was back outside, she found Imogen sitting in the passenger's seat of the Subaru, looking polished and ready to conquer the day.

Harlow climbed into the Subaru and glanced down at the jeans and plain black T-shirt she was wearing and wished she'd taken the time to dress a little more professionally. Or had her hair done any time in the past six months. Goddess knew she could use a cut and color. Next to her sister, she looked like someone in serious need of a makeover.

"Harlow, what are you waiting for?" Imogen asked, clearly frustrated that they weren't on the road yet.

"Sorry." Harlow put the car in gear and took off. Once they were on the main road, she held the pastry bag up. "Want one?"

"No thanks. I'm too nervous to eat."

Harlow shrugged. "Your loss."

By the time they made it to the winery, Harlow had eaten both pastries. Clearly, skipping both dinner *and* breakfast in favor of her time with Cash had left her famished.

"You have glaze on your face," Imogen said and then hopped out of the SUV.

Harlow lowered the visor to look in the mirror and let out a chuckle. Sure enough, she looked like a five-year-old who'd yet to master the art of using a napkin. Once she was cleaned up, she found her sister and another woman who looked like an older version of Hanna Pelsh standing just outside of a large barn.

"Hello, you must be Harlow." The woman held her hand out. "I'm Mary Pelsh."

"Mary, hi, it's nice to finally meet you," Harlow said, shaking her hand. "And to finally get out here to see your winery. It's just as gorgeous as Hanna said."

"Thank you. That's very kind." Mary spread her arms out wide. "Are you two ready for the tour?"

"Absolutely," Imogen said and fell into step beside the older woman.

Harlow trailed behind them, taking in the rows and rows of grapes with the mountains as a backdrop. No doubt this was the perfect setting for a wedding. The pictures would be to die for. As they made their way through the barn, Mary told them the space could be used for the ceremony or the reception or both. She went through the options of other alternative event spaces outside, with or without a tent. Then they chatted briefly about the vendors that they and their clients had used and the experiences they'd had.

Harlow had no earthly idea why Imogen needed her there. Her sister was killing the meeting. She was knowledgeable about the industry and exuded self-confidence.

With nothing interesting to contribute, Harlow started to daydream about her own wedding that she and Cash would have one day. It wasn't a matter of if; it was when. She knew that when they got around to discussing it again, she'd be all in and nothing would stop her from saying "I do" to him this time. She imagined a fall wedding ceremony with the vines heavy with grapes, ready to be harvested. It would be a smallish affair, intimate, with a party afterward at Equinox. Happiness filled her soul, and she couldn't help the smile tugging at her lips.

"Harlow?" The sound of her sister's insistent tone told Harlow that maybe it wasn't the first time Imogen had tried to get her attention.

"Huh?" Harlow asked, spinning around to face her and the amused Mary Pelsh.

"Mary offered us the use of their four-wheelers so we could take a quick trip along the horseless carriage trail," Imogen said. "Are you up for that?"

"Sure. But horseless carriage trail? What's that?"

"It's an enchantment we use for special events," Mary said. "Weddings, fall harvest, pumpkin fest, even Christmas. That kind of thing. We have a trail on the property and magical spots along the way that add to the experience. Most of it isn't spelled right now, but to give you some examples, in the past we've had animated snowmen, enchanted fireflies, and a magical skating rink that stays frozen year-round for those who like to have blades strapped to their feet. It's not my thing, but people seem to like it."

Harlow laughed. "I'm with you, Mary. If the skates were enchanted to keep me upright, I might consider it."

"Oh, they are," Mary said with a nod. "It just gets too cold for me. You two are welcome to try it out if you have time." She pointed to the back of the barn. "The four-wheelers are back there. Keys are in them already. See you soon. If your client shows up before you're back, I'll look after her."

"Enchanted skates," Harlow said, shaking her head. "I was just joking about that. Can you imagine? Maybe that's how the Olympians stay upright after flying through the air while doing their triple loops or whatever those jumps are called."

"I'm fairly certain all forms of magic are prohibited for the Olympics, Harlow," Imogen said, sounding amused.

"Right. Of course." Harlow grinned at her sister. "Are you going to try it?"

"Maybe another time. Right now, I want to stay focused."

"Gotcha."

When they were settled on the four-wheelers, Imogen took off, waving a hand for Harlow to follow her. There was a very clearly marked path starting behind the barn that ran the length of the grape vines and eventually disappeared into a thicket of trees. Everything was lush and smelled like she imagined heaven would smell.

She knew it must be one fantastic ride in a horseless carriage. Very romantic and preferable to the four-wheelers, but time was of the essence. Imogen's client would be there shortly.

The trail gave way to a meadow that was filled with spring wildflowers, and the sight nearly took Harlow's breath away.

Imogen slowed to a stop at the top of a small hill and leaned forward, gazing at the beauty.

Harlow joined her, and at the same time, they both said, "This is the perfect ceremony spot."

They looked at each other and burst out laughing.

"I guess things don't change after all," Harlow said. "We still share a brain sometimes."

"We do." Imogen slipped off her four-wheeler and walked to the edge of the hill. Without warning, she raised her arms and called, "*Papilionibus!*"

Almost instantly, three electric-blue butterflies appeared and fluttered around Imogen.

At the same time, the hair stood up on the back of Harlow's neck and a wave of nausea hit her. She instantly reached for the iron stake strapped to her leg. She couldn't see it, but she sure could feel it.

A spirit had arrived. And not a friendly one.

"Imogen! Look out!" Harlow cried the moment the spirit materialized, sending the blue butterflies scattering.

Imogen ducked, just in time to avoid being decked by a fallen log. The spirit that was standing near it snarled and went after her again, only this time, Harlow was there, her spike piercing the dark energy right where its heart would be. The spirit froze in place, unable to move as long as Harlow had a hold of the spike.

"Who are you?" Harlow demanded.

The spirit snarled.

"Eloquent," she said sarcastically. "Why are you attacking my sister?"

The spirit said nothing, continuing to stare at Imogen, seemingly obsessed with her.

"Harlow?" Imogen asked in a shaky voice. "Why is that thing here?"

"I don't know. It doesn't appear to be mentally capable enough to communicate with us." That happened sometimes when a spirit spent too much time suspended between worlds. "Give me a second. I'll get rid of it."

Harlow chanted an incantation, and when magic filled her fingers, she twisted the spike. Her magic poured into the spike and into the spirit. A few seconds later, the spirit started to pulse and then eventually shattered into a million little particles and disappeared into thin air.

"What in the hell?" Imogen raged, her face red and her fists balled. "Why am I always the target?"

Harlow didn't point out that she and Cash had been targets more times than she could count, wisely keeping that thought to herself. But they'd *willingly* put themselves in those positions. Imogen was just practicing a spell for butterflies.

Then it hit her. That was the second time in two days when Imogen had cast a spell and a spirit appeared. She bit down on her bottom lip. Was it possible that Imogen's magic was summoning spirits?

"Gen," Harlow said tentatively.

"What?" Imogen was scowling and looked like she was ready to tear her hair out.

"Yesterday when you were practicing Gran's spells out in the forest behind the house, did you notice anything unusual happening?"

"Huh?" she asked, clearly taken off guard. Then Harlow's question registered, and she shook her head. "No, not that I noticed. Why?"

"Both last night and today, as soon as you cast a spell, a spirit showed up. I was just wondering if the two things were connected."

"That's ridiculous," Imogen said, dismissing the theory immediately. "A lot of people were casting spells last night, including you. How do we know it's not you who's attracting them?"

Harlow could point out that she hadn't used any magic that day but didn't. It was entirely possible that Harlow was the magnet. She had been in the past and likely would be in the future. But her gut was telling her it was Imogen, and if there was one thing Harlow had learned in all her years of hunting ghosts, it was that she had to trust her gut. "I don't think it's me," Harlow said. "But we can't be sure." She reached over and squeezed her sister's hand. "Please just be careful, okay? I worry about you."

Imogen's shoulders were stiff, and there was fire in her eyes when she said, "I'm always careful. Let's go. Sadie will be here any minute."

Harlow watched as her sister climbed on the four-wheeler and took off back toward the winery. She glanced around one last time and opened up her senses, trying to see if she could connect with any spirits. Nothing. Whatever that thing had been, it was gone, and all that remained was a gorgeous, peaceful wildflower garden.

CHAPTER 21

*W*hen Harlow finally caught up to her sister, Imogen had already parked the four-wheeler and was striding into the barn. Harlow could tell by her gait that she was flustered, and Harlow prayed she was able to put the spirit out of her mind while she talked to her new client.

"How was the ride?" Mary Pelsh asked, appearing from the barn.

"It was gorgeous," Harlow said, giving her a small smile. Then she grimaced. "Right up until a spirit attacked Imogen."

"What?" Mary's dark eyes widened in utter shock. "What spirit? Was she hurt?"

"No. I was able to dispel the spirit before anything terrible happened."

"Thank the goddess!" Mary said, placing a hand on her heart. "I just don't know what I'd do if that happened to one of our guests. Is there some way to ward off those things? Is there something we should be doing to protect the property?"

"There are things you can do," Harlow said, taking the woman's hand and squeezing it, immediately falling back into her ghost hunter persona she'd shunned for the last year. "But before you get too worried, let me ask you some questions."

"Of course." Mary stared at the trail as if waiting for a spirit to appear.

"Have you ever seen a ghost on your property before?"

"No, never." She shook her head. "But I'm not a medium, either."

"Has anyone else ever seen a ghost here that you're aware of?"

"Not that I'm aware of, no," Mary said.

Harlow sucked in a breath and let it out slowly. "That's what I was afraid of."

"Explain," Mary said, studying her intently.

"It appears that either I or my sister attracted that spirit. I don't think there's any reason to believe that this property is haunted." Harlow looked around at the serene vineyard. "If strange, unexplainable things haven't been happening, then I'd chalk this up to a Thane sister issue for now."

"You're sure?" Mary asked, studying Harlow. "If anyone gets hurt here, I'll never forgive myself."

"I'd bet money on it, but if you ever want to cleanse the property or put in protection wards, Cash and I can help you with that. Just let me know."

"Okay. Thanks. That's reassuring. I'll talk it over with Walter and see if we have extra funds in the budget for that sort of thing. Do you have a ballpark range?"

"Oh no!" Harlow said quickly. "I'm sorry. I wasn't clear. There wouldn't be any charge for that. I'd just want to make sure your property wasn't susceptible to more unwanted ghosts. That's all."

Mary smiled at her. "That's very kind of you. Thank you."

"It's no problem at all." Harlow knew that if more spirits

started showing up after today, it was likely that either she or Imogen had opened a door to the spirit world that she hadn't closed when she'd banished the spirit that attacked Imogen. If that was the case, she'd for sure need to cast some protections spells. But usually if a door or portal was opened, ghosts started to show up right away, and so far they hadn't. It didn't look like the Pelshes had anything to worry about. "Thanks for the information, Mary. I'm going to go find Imogen. Give me a call if you need me."

"I will."

Harlow made her way back into the barn, and when she didn't see Imogen or anyone else, she checked on the front patio. She immediately spotted her sister and a pretty blonde she recognized to be Sadie Lewis. They were sitting on some patio furniture under an awning to her right.

Even before Harlow reached them, she could tell that her sister was on edge. Tension lined her face, and she kept diverting her focus from the blonde in order to scan her surroundings as if she were waiting for the other shoe to drop.

"I have refreshments," a woman said from behind Harlow.

Turning, Harlow spotted Candy Pelsh, Hanna's cousin who also worked at Incantation Café. "Candy, hi."

"Hey, Harlow. Beautiful day, isn't it?"

"It is."

They joined Imogen and Sadie. Candy handed wine to Sadie and what looked like lemonade to Imogen. She glanced at Harlow. "Did you want anything? We have wine, cider, beer, water, lemonade, and soft drinks."

"I'm fine," Harlow said, sitting next to her sister.

The tension radiating off Imogen made Harlow's stomach clench. She wished there was something she could do for her, but other than whisking her away to the spa, she didn't know what that might be.

"So, I like the idea of having the ceremony outside, but even in June, you never can be sure about rain around here, so I'm not sure it's a good idea," Sadie said to Imogen. "And if it's inside, I think the barn is really overkill. We'll only have about a dozen people."

"The barn is pretty big for that," Imogen said and then listed a bunch of places in town that might be more appropriate for the small wedding party. Most of them were restaurants, but then she said, "I think if it's in the budget, how about A Touch of Magic Day Spa? I've heard they have a covered patio out back that is gorgeous."

"I like that idea," Sadie said, studying Imogen. Her brows were pinched, and she looked like something was bothering her, but she never said as much. Instead, she appeared to be fully engaged in the conversation. In no time at all, they'd worked out a game plan to see the spa and had a list of restaurants that would work for a small reception.

"Do you have any hobbies, Imogen?" Sadie suddenly asked her out of the blue.

"Hobbies?" Imogen was completely taken off guard as she looked up at the woman. "Why do you ask?"

Sadie shrugged. "Just curious. You seem a little tense today. I was trying to loosen you up a little."

"Oh, I'm so sorry," Imogen said. "I hope I didn't make you uncomfortable. We had an... *unusual* morning today, and I think I'm just still trying to process it all."

That was one way to put it. Still, Harlow was proud of her sister for her professional demeanor.

"No, no. I'm not uncomfortable," Sadie said, putting her at

ease. "That's not it at all. I was just trying to help. I'm sorry if I overstepped."

"You didn't," Imogen reassured her. "As far as hobbies go, I don't have many. I've moved too many times the past couple of years. Things have been kind of up in the air." She glanced at Harlow. "But I'm hoping I can put down roots now. I'm thinking of taking up hiking now that I live so close to all this beauty."

Harlow could see that the conversation was helping Imogen, but her eyes were still narrowed, and she was clutching her notebook so hard that her knuckles had turned white.

"The hiking around here is great. If you ever need a hiking buddy, I'm available," Sadie said.

"I'm not." Candy let out a laugh. "I gave that up a few years back after I sprained my ankle. Now I stick to walks along the river, and I've taken up crocheting."

"You have?" Harlow asked. "Are you taking lessons at Zya's shop?"

"I am. So far, I've made three scarves and a cowl. It's great in the winter. Now that it's spring, we'll see how we do once it gets warmer here."

"I want to learn pottery," Harlow said. "If I could find a teaching studio somewhere close by."

Sadie gave her the name of a studio in Eureka.

The four of them talked about various hobbies and activities for a while until Sadie stood and said, "I better get going before I'm late for my shift at the brewery. Imogen, you'll give me a call about the estimate and a time we can get together again to finalize details?"

"Absolutely." Imogen stood and shook the woman's hand.

"Thank you for trusting me with this. It's not every day someone's willing to take a chance on a new business."

Sadie laughed. "I'm sure whatever you do will be infinitely better than what I could come up with. Weddings, while lovely to attend sometimes, just aren't something I've ever dreamed about."

Candy let out an exaggerated sigh. "Oh, I do. One day some hot guy is going to walk into town and sweep me off my feet, and then the wedding will be epic."

Imogen chuckled. "I hope you'll give me a call to help you with the planning."

"Are you sure you want to deal with all of this?" Candy waved a hand in front of her own face and laughed. "I've been told I can be a little... particular."

Sadie snickered. "More like demanding and unreasonable."

"Well, that was just rude," Candy said, casting her a mock-offended look.

"Tell me I'm wrong," Sadie challenged.

"No way. You just didn't have to say it like that." They both cracked up.

Harlow grinned at them, enjoying watching their banter. It was one of the things she loved about the town. The people were fun and truly seemed to love each other.

The three of them waved goodbye to Sadie as she retreated to her car. Imogen asked Candy to thank her aunt and uncle for her and said she couldn't wait to hold an event there someday soon.

As soon as Imogen and Harlow were on their way back to the Subaru, Imogen tensed again.

"Hey, what's wrong?" Harlow asked.

"I just can't shake the feeling that I've done something to

deserve the wrath of these spirits." There was a tremble in her voice when she added, "Why are they coming after me?"

"It's not you, Gen," Harlow said, wrapping an arm around her shoulder. "Sometimes spirits just look for an opening. You absolutely didn't do anything wrong."

She shook her head. "It doesn't feel that way."

Harlow wasn't sure what to say. She didn't have answers for her sister. Neither of them could know what was going on unless they started digging around, and she was certain Imogen didn't want her messing with more ghosts.

A red Toyota Camry was parked a few spaces from Harlow's Subaru. As they passed by, Sadie waved through the open window and started the engine. As soon as the music came on, Sadie started to sing along.

A faint trace of magic tickled Harlow's skin and she spun, looking to see who'd cast a spell. But when Sadie backed out and sped out of the parking lot, the magic vanished. "Did you feel that?" Harlow asked Imogen.

Imogen was staring after the Camry, her eyes wide. "She fixed me."

"What?"

"The anxiousness that had me all tensed up," Imogen said. "Sadie fixed me. I don't know how, but she did. That magic was coming from her, right?"

Harlow nodded, still trying to wrap her head around what her sister was saying. "I don't understand, Imogen. What do you mean she fixed you?"

Imogen turned to her, an easy smile lighting up her entire face. "Ever since last year, when Crazy Cora possessed me, it takes almost nothing at all to get my anxiety into overdrive. I've been battling it all morning since that spirit showed up here. But suddenly, after whatever Sadie did, it's gone. I feel like a heavy blanket has been lifted off me." She let out a small laugh. "Like I've lost ten pounds, instantly."

Harlow had no idea what just happened, but she didn't even care. All that mattered was that her sister was feeling better, and for that she was grateful. Harlow opened her arms and gave her sister a tight hug. "We'll need to send her a thank you basket."

"If this holds out, I'm thinking monthly ones," Imogen said, squeezing just as hard. When she released Harlow, she asked, "What do you think she did?"

"Beats me. We can ask her later, though. Right now, I'm thinking coffee and lunch. What do you think about inviting Cash and Shaun?"

"Sounds perfect," Imogen said, unable to keep a stupid grin off her face.

Harlow noticed her giddiness but kept her thoughts to herself. If Imogen was happy, that was all that mattered.

Just as they climbed into the SUV, Imogen's phone buzzed with a text. "It's the Mustang. It's fixed already."

"Perfect. We'll go pick it up, drop this one off at home, take it for a spin, and then meet the boys at the Keating Hollow Brewery. Cam is opening the pub today, so I don't have to be there until later this afternoon."

Imogen nodded and then texted Shaun. *Lunch at Keating Hollow Brewery with you and Cash. Meet us in an hour.*

The response was almost immediate. *We'll be there.*

CHAPTER 22

"We've been summoned for lunch," Shaun said as he walked out of the parlor that he'd established as his office, adjacent to the front room.

"Really? By whom?" Cash asked as he went back to studying the plans he'd made for remodeling the primary bathroom.

"The Good Witch of the West," he said sarcastically. "Who do you think summoned us?"

Cash glanced up at his brother and laughed at the annoyance on his face. "Well, I wasn't sure because normally I'd assume Harlow or Imogen. But if it were Harlow, no doubt she'd contact me. And since you haven't told me one single thing about your relationship with Imogen, I wasn't sure if you had *that* kind of relationship. So I thought I'd better ask."

"Smartass. You know I spent the night with Imogen last night. Of course it was her. And Harlow is with her. They want us to meet them at the brewery in an hour."

"Cool. I could use a beer," Cash said and grinned because he didn't give one damn about the beer. He was just happy to see Harlow so soon after she'd left that morning.

"You're a goner. You know that?" Shaun asked him. "It's seriously disturbing to see you with that starry-eyed look on your face."

"Get used to it, brother. It's not going away any time soon… if ever," Cash said with a laugh.

Shaun groaned.

"Don't knock it till you try it." He gave his brother his full attention. "And don't think I didn't notice how you sidestepped my comment about Imogen. Are you ready to tell me what's up between you two?"

"Nope." Shaun turned around and walked back into his office. Before he shut the door, he called, "I'll be ready to go in forty-five minutes."

"I'll be right here," Cash called back and shook his head. He didn't know why his brother was being so tight-lipped about Imogen. Cash obviously knew he was spending a bunch of time with her and that she'd invited him to lunch. It was clearly more than a booty call. What was wrong with just saying they were seeing each other? He guessed he'd know more at lunch.

Just before it was time to go meet the girls in town, Cash got up and headed into the kitchen. As he was pouring himself a glass of water, the air shimmered beside him and Aunt Jane appeared. She didn't look at him. She just stared out the window, a frown on her face. "Aunt Jane?" he asked.

Her eyes seemed unfocused, and her spirit form flickered as if she were having trouble maintaining her presence.

"Aunt Jane, what's wrong?"

"There's trouble, Cash," she said, her voice grave. "Trouble is coming." Her image flickered out, and then she was gone.

"Aunt Jane?" Cash called, his heart suddenly thumping rapidly against his ribcage. "Come back!" He strode from the room, into the dining room, and all over the first floor of the house. Then he ran upstairs looking for her, but she didn't reappear.

Her words echoed in his mind as he ran back downstairs, calling, "Shaun, we have to go. Now."

When his brother didn't respond, Cash rushed into his office and stopped dead in his tracks.

Shaun was sitting rigid in his chair, his eyes closed as they moved back and forth rapidly as if he were in REM sleep. But Cash knew better. His brother was in the middle of a vision. The only thing to do was wait it out.

"Dammit," he muttered and reached for his phone. With a tap, he called Harlow, but the call went straight to voice mail. He tried again with the same result. He gripped the phone so hard his hand started to ache.

Shaun slumped in his chair and let out a groan.

"Shaun? What did you see?" Cash asked as he kneeled in front of his brother.

"It's Harlow. She's in that same house with the modern appliances that I saw before. That vision I had of you that never came true. She's there, and she's not herself. It's as if… I don't know. She's just not herself. She's preening and acting like a diva, something she never does." He grabbed his head and winced. "It's too much. That one gave me a massive headache."

"We'll grab you some ibuprofen on the way out. We have to go. Now," Cash said, already pulling his brother up out of the chair.

"Go where?" Shaun asked, frowning in concentration.

"We need to find Harlow and Imogen," Cash said impatiently. He knew his brother was always a little out of it after his visions and usually needed to rest a bit, but there just wasn't any time for that.

"I'm not going to lunch," Shaun said, sounding more like himself already.

"We're not going to lunch. We're going to go find Harlow and Imogen. They are in danger."

"Danger?" Shaun rubbed the back of his neck. "How?"

He tugged his brother out of the chair and hauled him into the kitchen to get him painkillers and water as he explained what Aunt Jane told him during her brief appearance. Once they were out of the house, Cash asked, "Do you have your phone?"

"Yeah." Shaun patted his pocket.

"Call Imogen. See if you can get her on the phone."

He frowned. "We usually text."

"Then text, but if she doesn't reply right away, you have to call her," Cash insisted as they got into his Jeep. "Gods. Why are people so phone averse these days?"

Shaun didn't bother to answer. He sent a few texts, and when there were no replies, he called. "It went straight to voice mail."

Cash let out a small growl and tightened his grip on the steering wheel. "Why are both of their phones going straight to voice mail?"

"They're probably out of the service area," Shaun said in a far too reasonable tone.

"You're not worried at all?" Cash asked him as he sped toward town.

"I'm a little worried. Aunt Jane's warning and my premonition aren't good signs. But I prefer to panic when we're certain there's actually something to panic about."

"Since when did you become so level-headed?" Cash muttered but didn't expect an answer. Nor did he get one.

They were silent for the rest of the way to town, but when they came to a stop in the parking lot of the Keating Hollow Brewery, Shaun said, "They're not here."

"How do you know?" Cash was already out of the Jeep and was leaning down to stare at his brother.

"Neither of their cars are here." Shaun fiddled with his phone as if he were searching for something.

"I'm going to run in and make sure." Cash didn't wait for his response. He was far too worried about Harlow to care if his brother got annoyed at being left in the car.

The brewery was only moderately busy. One glance around the dining room and he knew that Harlow wasn't there. He walked up to the bar and gestured to the woman behind the counter.

"What can I get you to drink?" the petite blonde asked with a wide smile.

"Nothing today. I'm looking for someone. Actually two someones. Harlow and Imogen Thane. They—"

"Oh, I did see them today," she said with a nod. "I met with them this morning. Both of them are really lovely people. I'm looking forward to working with Imogen. I just can't deal with my cousin's wedding. Talk about a bridezilla. The wedding dress drama alone, I mean—"

"I'm sorry," Cash said, cutting off her rambling. "Where and when did you see them?"

"Oh, this morning out at the Pelsh winery. Imogen is the new wedding planner for my cousin's wedding."

Cash nodded. "Okay, that's a start. But they haven't been in here today?"

She shook her head. "No. I would have definitely noticed. Why? Are they supposed to be here?"

"We were meeting them for lunch, but they seem to have run into some sort of a snag. Listen, uh, what did you say your name is?" Cash asked her.

"I didn't, but it's Sadie," she said.

"It's nice to meet you, Sadie. I'm Cash. If I leave you my business card, can you call me if you see either of them?"

She frowned, looking torn. "You don't just want me to tell them to call you?"

"Yes, I'd love it if they'd call, but if for some reason they can't, will you please let me know if you see them?"

"I don't know you, Cash..." She stared at the card he'd dropped on the counter. When she looked up, she said, "Cash Moses. Anyway, I'm not in the business of giving away people's locations when they don't want to be found."

It took every bit of control Cash had not to lash out at the woman. He sucked in a long breath and said, "I appreciate that. But all I'm trying to do is make sure my girl and her sister are safe."

"Then you'll be fine if they call you," she said with a shrug and started to wipe down the counter.

"Fine," Cash said, ready to throttle someone. "Just tell them that Shaun and I are worried, okay?"

"Of course." Sadie smiled, looking very pleased with herself. "Now, what can I get you to drink?"

Cash just shook his head and walked out.

When he reached the Jeep, Shaun said, "No luck?"

"None whatsoever." Cash climbed into the Jeep, pulled out his phone, and checked Harlow's location.

Nothing. Her dot didn't register at all.

He wanted to scream.

CHAPTER 23

"Thank you for paying for the repairs," Imogen said as she and Harlow walked out of the repair shop. "I'll pay you back as soon as I can."

"Don't worry about it." Harlow moved to stand next to the Mustang and ran a hand over the fender. "It's good to have you back, baby," she whispered to the vehicle. She glanced up at her sister. "A car her age always takes a little extra care. Let's get her home so we can meet the boys for lunch."

Imogen handed her the car keys. "You drive her. I'll take your Subaru."

"I'm not going to say no to that." Harlow jumped into the Mustang and fired her up. All the way back to the house, the car ran beautifully and handled like a dream. Her blood hummed with contentment, and pure joy filled her heart at being back behind the wheel of the car she and Cash had loved so much. She couldn't believe she'd actually sold it.

She'd made the excuse that Celia wasn't practical for the Keating Hollow winters, but truthfully, there had just been too many painful memories. She'd done what she'd needed to at the time, but now that she and Cash were back together, she wanted the car back, too. She made up her mind that she'd offer to buy her sister a newer car in exchange for the Mustang. Then she could feel the hum of the muscle car beneath her bones any time she wanted.

When they got back to the house, Harlow didn't cut the engine. She just waited patiently for her sister to park, run into the house to use the facilities, and then finally come back out and get into the passenger seat. Imogen barely had her seatbelt buckled when Harlow took off again.

"Where are you going?" Imogen asked with a laugh when Harlow turned right instead of left. "Downtown is the other way."

"I wanna take this baby out and see what she can do. We have some time before we're supposed to meet the boys. You okay with that?"

"Sure," Imogen said, chuckling. "You always did handle this car better than me."

"About that." Harlow glanced at her sister. "I think I'm ready to buy her back from you. How about we go car shopping sometime this week and find you something reliable that you love?"

Imogen's smile vanished. "I'd love to, Harlow, but I'm not ready to make payments. I was hoping to get my business established and then—"

"You don't understand," Harlow said. "I'll buy the car and we'll just swap."

"But that's not a fair trade," she said, frowning.

"Sure it is. Have you looked up how much these things are worth? I'm sure we can find you something great."

Imogen blinked at her. "More than what I paid for it last year?"

Harlow nodded. "Yep. A lot more."

"But…" Imogen narrowed her eyes at her sister. "You're saying you gave me a sweetheart deal? Why, guilt?"

"Yes and no." Harlow turned the car onto a stretch of road that was outside of town and rarely used because there were only a few houses at the end of the ten-mile stretch. "I couldn't drive her anymore for personal reasons, but I didn't want to see her go to someone else. So I sold Celia to you for cheap to keep her in the family. Now I'm ready to buy her back. But it's not your problem I'm a terrible negotiator." Harlow winked. "So I'll buy you something that's roughly on par with Celia's value, and I'll take her back. It's a win for us both."

Imogen scoffed. "That's absurd. I can't let you do that."

"Sure you can. There's nothing wrong with letting me use some of my ghost-hunting money to help my sister out, is there?"

"No, but I don't want to be a charity case." Imogen crossed her arms over her chest. "I'm not here just because I had nowhere to go, you know. I missed my sister. Not her bank account."

A lump formed in Harlow's throat, and she had to fight off tears. It was exactly what she needed to hear from her sister. She reached over and squeezed Imogen's hand before she forced out, "I missed you, too. Please just let me do this. After everything we've both been through, I don't want money to be an issue, too. I want the Mustang; you want something more reliable. I can make that happen. It's not a bribe or something I'm doing because I think I owe you. I just want to make it easier for you to start your life here. That's all."

Imogen's eyes misted, and she did nothing to try to stop the few tears that rolled down her cheeks. "Okay. If you're sure."

"I'm sure," Harlow said. "Tomorrow. We'll make it happen."

Imogen grinned. "Sounds like a plan. Now let's see what this machine can do."

"Gladly!" Harlow stepped on the gas, and the two of them let out a whoop of joy as they flew down the road.

Harlow was in her element. Despite the worries about the spirits that seemed to be popping up recently, everything was falling into place. Cash was back in her life. She and her sister were rebuilding their relationship. And she was reunited with her first love, her Mustang, Celia.

Life was just about as perfect as she could hope for.

Right up until the Mustang sputtered and jerked and then died.

Harlow and Imogen looked at each other, both of them speechless.

Finally Harlow said, "Well, that sucks."

"Majorly," Imogen agreed.

Then they both reached for their phones.

"I don't have a signal," Harlow said. "Do you?"

"Nope." Imogen climbed out of the Mustang and started moving the phone around in the air, trying to find a signal.

Harlow joined her, and when neither of them accessed any cell service, Harlow stuffed her phone in her pocket and said, "Well, I guess it's time to get walking."

Imogen groaned. "And here I thought things were going better."

Chuckling, Harlow said, "I was just thinking that when the car broke down. Maybe I jinxed us."

"Oh, so it's your fault," Imogen said with a teasing tone.

"Looks like it." Harlow stood on the road and glanced around, trying to figure out the best course of action.

"There's a house up there," Imogen said, pointing to a house on the side of the hill. She squinted. "Looks like maybe that's the road to it."

"If they have a landline, that would work," Harlow said. "They'd probably have to if there's no cell service here, right?"

"Probably. Or wi-fi. If it's password protected, that could be a problem."

Harlow thought it over and said, "We could try that option first. And if it doesn't work out, we'll head to town. What do you think?"

"Yeah, okay."

After Harlow locked the Mustang, the pair of them headed up the steep road. By the time they reached the driveway, they were both clutching their chests and barely able to breathe.

"I think I'm going to die," Imogen gasped out.

"You've made it this far. Stay with me," Harlow panted.

"I'll try."

Harlow led the way up the stairs to the beautiful, modern house. She wasted no time knocking on the door.

"It's just our luck no one is here," Imogen said, sounding defeated. "I can't believe we climbed that mountain just to find the house empty."

Harlow chuckled. "Mountain? It wasn't that intense."

"It felt like it."

"Don't give up yet." Harlow peeked in the windows. No one appeared to be around. But she did see a landline phone sitting on an end table in the living room. "Jackpot. There's a phone."

Imogen joined her, looking in the window. "It doesn't do us much good if there's no one here to let us in."

"True." Harlow chewed on her bottom lip. "Let's go around back and just make sure there's really no one here."

"You're trying to kill me, aren't you?" Imogen complained.

"Nah. I just got you back. Why would I do that?"

Imogen gave her a hint of a smile and followed her around the property.

As it turned out, there wasn't any sign of life. It was hard to say, but Harlow guessed that maybe it was a second home that wasn't lived in full time. It just didn't look like anyone had settled in.

"Okay, enough of this. There's a phone in that living room, and I vote we just go in and use it," Imogen said.

"You mean break in?" Harlow asked her sister, both eyebrows raised in question.

"Not exactly. I mean, we won't be breaking anything. Or stealing anything. We're in an emergency situation. It's warranted, right?"

Harlow wasn't sure it was exactly an emergency situation, but they were about ten miles away from town and it wasn't like they'd seen another car on the road they'd taken. Walking back to town would take three or four hours, and part of that would mean walking along a two-lane highway. She didn't love the idea of trespassing, but the alternative wasn't attractive either. "Okay, we'll try to find a way in, use the phone, and then leave everything the way we found it."

Imogen nodded, reached for the knob on the back door, and, without warning, hit it with a bolt of magic. The shimmering light wrapped around it and seeped into the crack at the doorframe. An instant later, Harlow heard the slide of the dead bolt. Imogen grinned at her and then walked in the back door.

Harlow glanced around one last time, praying they weren't caught on any security cameras, and then followed her sister into the house.

Instantly, the door slammed shut and the wind picked up, roaring through the house, sending a clock from the wall flying. Harlow ducked and it flew over her head, crashing into the wall behind her. "Imogen!" Harlow cried. "We have to get out of here."

But there was no answer.

Harlow glanced around, frantic to find her sister through the flying debris. She wasn't in the kitchen. Inching forward with her head down, Harlow slowly made her way to the living room. Once she stepped through the door, the wind intensified.

Harlow could barely see through the tears caused by the wind, but then she blinked and saw Imogen right in the middle of the room, her face frozen in horror.

"Imogen!" Harlow cried. "What is it?"

Her sister stared right at her and mouthed, *Cora is here.*

CHAPTER 24

"No!" Harlow cried and lunged toward her sister.

A lamp flew across the room, barely missing Harlow's head by mere inches. Somewhere in the back of her mind, Harlow registered that there was no way they were leaving the house the way they'd found it. The moment Imogen doubled over as if she'd been punched in the gut, all thoughts of the house vanished from her mind.

"Leave her alone!" Harlow cried, wishing she'd thought to bring any of her ghost-hunting supplies. She didn't even have a bag of salt to try to trap the spirit. Her only hope was her iron spike and her magic, and neither of those had worked against Cora before.

With her spike in one hand and magic sparking at the tips of her fingers on the other, Harlow slashed the air around her, hoping she'd somehow wound the ghost she couldn't see. She reached Imogen's side and leaned down to stare her in the eyes. "Are you okay?"

Imogen shook her head, tears standing in her eyes as she held her abdomen. "I feel like I'm going to throw up."

"But you're still *you*, right? What was the name of your first Barbie?" Harlow doubted the spirit could access Imogen's memories from that long ago and was banking on the idea that this would tell her if her sister was already possessed.

"Baldy," Imogen gasped.

"Good job." Harlow gave her a grim smile and then stood, shielding her sister. "If you want a fight, Crazy Cora, you've got one."

The lights flickered on and off and Harlow took that as challenge accepted. The air turned thick as magic coated Harlow's skin and she just knew that the spirit was near. She might not be able to see her, but she sure as hell could feel her. "Imogen, get back!" Harlow ordered as she slashed the air with her spike and sent a bolt of magic out toward the disturbing energy.

All it did was hit a framed picture on the wall and shatter it.

"Dammit!" Harlow cried.

That awful wind intensified and was swirling with such pressure that Harlow could barely move. It was as if the spirit was using the elements to bind her in place. That was something she could combat at least. Instead of focusing on the spirit, she changed her focus to the wind and sent a stream of magic straight into the vortex swirling around her.

There was an instant tug on her power and Harlow felt her control slipping. Sweat popped out on her forehead as she battled it, but just when she thought she might not win this war, finally her magic broke through and the wind came to a sudden stop.

"Harlow?" Imogen said, her voice sounding very small and very scared.

And that's when she finally saw an outline of the ghost she'd been battling in one way or another for over a year. She was standing over Imogen's prone form, one hand already fused with Imogen's. She was trying to possess Harlow's sister again, and Harlow knew if that happened it was likely Imogen would be lost to her forever.

"Not today, Satan!" Harlow cried and ran toward the spirit, diving right into her. The transformation was instantaneous. A sadistic joy ran through her as the spirit made her home in Harlow's body. She stood tall and looked at the world through her new eyes and gave Imogen a sickly-sweet smile.

"Hey, sis," the spirit said, keeping Harlow locked away in a corner of her mind. "Crazy Cora is gone. How about you give Cash a call so he can pick us up?"

Imogen stared at her with suspicious eyes. "Harlow?"

"Yeah?"

"What happened to Cora?"

"She's gone," Cora said. "She's no match for my magic. Are you ready to get out of here or not?"

She'll see right through you, Harlow told the spirit. *My sister isn't an idiot.*

True, Cora said. *She's actually much quicker than you are.* She tsked. *It took you forever to realize your sister wasn't herself. But I've learned from that experience. If I act like you, I can just take over your life. Plus, you're the one with all the money. I don't know why I didn't pick you as a host in the first place.*

Imogen stared at Cora, her brows pinched. "She's really gone? How did you get rid of her?"

Cora made a confused face. "You know, I'm not really sure. Maybe it was my magic and my spike combined." She reached down to pick up the iron spike, but as soon as she did, she pulled her hand back and dropped it as she hissed, "Holy mother of slug slime."

"Slug slime?" Imogen narrowed her eyes. "Since when did you pick up that saying?"

"Since now. Make the call so we can get out of here," Cora snapped.

Harlow knew that her sister would see right through Cora. Or at least she hoped she would.

But when Imogen nodded and moved to pick up the phone, Harlow's heart sank. Maybe she hadn't realized that she was talking to Cora and now Harlow was going to be trapped in her own mind forever. *Cash will notice. You know that, right? He'll find a way to destroy you.*

Now there's a sexy piece of manmeat. I'm going to enjoy him thoroughly before I end him.

End him? Harlow shot back, panicked. *What the hell do you mean by that?*

I can't have him trying to rescue you, now can I? I'm sure he's fun in the sack and all, but there are other useful idiots for that particular activity. Like Shaun. He's just as pretty as his brother, and he's got that dominance thing about him in the bedroom. Hot.

Harlow mentally shuddered at the thought of what Crazy Cora had in store for the Moses boys. *I won't let anything happen to Cash,* Harlow warned the spirit.

It's not really up to you, now is it, Harlow?

It is if I say it is, Harlow said defiantly.

So much spunk. So entertaining. That's why I chose you as my next host instead of your sister.

You didn't choose me. I saved my sister from you, and you decided to take me instead, Harlow spat back.

That's what you think happened, anyway. Cora's smugness made Harlow want to throttle her. If only that didn't mean ringing her own neck.

"Shaun, Harlow and I need your help," Imogen said into the

phone as she stared at Cora. She explained how the Mustang broke down and that they were stranded. And then she said something odd. Something that gave Harlow hope. "Remember that time we were talking about the chaos of my grandmother's banana pudding recipe contest?"

Their grandmother had hated banana pudding and certainly would never organize a contest around it. She hadn't been a joiner anyway, but doing anything revolving around banana pudding would have made her gag.

There was a pause as Imogen listened to Shaun.

"No. It was Harlow's favorite, not mine," Imogen said. "Yes, that's right."

"Get on with it!" Cora warned. "You can small-talk your boy toy after they pick us up."

"Harlow's in a hurry," Imogen said into the phone. "Yes. Okay. I'll meet you down at the road." She hung up the phone and said, "They're on their way. Since I don't know the address, I'm going to meet them down there so they can find us."

"You didn't need to do that," Cora admonished her. "You could have just dropped them a pin to show where we are."

"How was I going to do that with no signal, *Harlow*?" Imogen stressed Harlow's name, confirming to her sister that she knew exactly what was going on. Harlow just didn't know what crazy plan she'd cooked up. She just prayed that Imogen wouldn't try to take on Cora without help.

Cora scowled at her and said, "Fine. I'll wait with you."

But Imogen shook her head. "You said you wanted to leave this place exactly as we found it. Don't you think it should at least be cleaned up? You start sweeping up the broken debris, and after the boys get here, we'll help with whatever is left."

"You want me to clean?" the spirit shot back, sounding incredulous.

"Why not? You told me the other day it was cathartic. Don't be so precious, Harlow. It's just a bit of sweeping." Imogen tossed her hair over her shoulder and walked out the front door.

Harlow wanted to stand up and applaud. She didn't know exactly what Imogen was up to, but she recognized that it was something. And that was just the piece of hope that kept her holding on even as Cora started in on how she was going to destroy everything Harlow loved. Starting with Cash.

Bite me, Harlow said. *You can try, but in the end, you'll go back to hell where you belong.*

The spirit let out a divisive, humorless laugh. "That's what they all say."

CHAPTER 25

"We have to go," Shaun said the moment he ended the call with Imogen. "It's Harlow. She's in trouble."

"What does that mean?" Cash demanded, already heading toward his Jeep. When they hadn't found Harlow and Imogen at the brewery, they'd gone to their house and found it empty. Harlow's Subaru was there, but the Mustang was gone. With no other leads, they'd gone downtown and started asking around to see if anyone had seen them. The answer had been a universal no.

"If I'm understanding Imogen's code correctly, she thinks that Harlow has been possessed," Shaun said.

Cash stopped dead in his tracks and turned to his brother. "Why would she think that? Harlow's never been possessed before. We're talking about the most powerful medium any of us have ever met."

"Whoa!" Shaun raised both hands. "I don't know anything other than Imogen was talking in code and said Harlow is in trouble. I don't have any other answers."

Cash stared at him for a long moment and then abruptly turned and quickened his pace to the Jeep. Once they were both in the vehicle, Cash slammed it into gear and looked at his brother. "Where is she?"

Shaun relayed the details of their location and held on as Cash did a quick U-turn right in front of another vehicle. The noise from the horn pierced the air, making Cash's ears ring, but he ignored it. His only focus was finding Harlow and making sure she was safe.

Once they sped out of town, Cash turned to his brother. "Tell me about this code. How do you know Imogen was trying to say Harlow was in trouble?"

"Oh, that." Shaun rubbed a hand down his face, looking grim. "The reason I haven't told you about my relationship with Imogen is because we started out as friends."

Cash gave him a confused look. "Of course you started out as friends. You've known each other for years."

"I know, but not like this." Shaun stared straight ahead and then continued talking. "After you and Harlow broke up, it felt to me like all of your lives had imploded. You and Harlow weren't talking. Harlow and Imogen were barely talking. You weren't talking to me and even though I wasn't a part of any of it, I just had a feeling that someone needed to reach out to Imogen to make sure she was okay. I don't know why exactly, I just did. So I called her."

"And?" Cash asked.

"And we became friends. Imogen almost never talked about the possession. She never gave details, and I didn't press her. But she did sometimes express worry about it happening again someday. I wasn't sure what to say about that. I did some research on spirit possession, but it seems like every case was different. The factors seemed to be how powerful the spirit was and if the person possessed had any magical ability and what kind."

"Okay, Shaun. Get to the point. How did you know that Imogen was speaking in code?" Cash asked impatiently.

"I read somewhere that sometimes the possessed could break the hold a spirit had on them and communicate with others. Imogen was skeptical because she said Crazy Cora always shut her down any time she tried to communicate to Harlow what was going on. So I told her to speak in code and made a silly comment about making banana pudding the code word. She laughed and said that while she and Harlow loved banana pudding, their grandmother never made it because she hated it with a passion. From there, it turned into a conversation about where to find the best banana pudding, and we never talked about it again."

"You're telling me that Imogen said something about banana pudding today? Wouldn't that imply that she's the one possessed?" Cash asked, eyeing his brother briefly as he sped down the curvy road.

"It could, but she was clear that it was Harlow that liked the pudding. I'm pretty sure that means Harlow is the one in trouble, and Imogen didn't want to tip the spirit off that she knew."

"That's a pretty good leap," Cash said, unable to even contemplate the idea that Harlow might be possessed by a ghost. She was far too strong and always had been. But it was true that she'd almost lost to Crazy Cora while exorcising her from Imogen the year before. If she was possessed it had to be Crazy Cora. No other ghost had come close to that much power. But why? And what was her obsession with the Thane sisters?

Cash's head started to ache from worry, and he pushed the

Jeep to the limits, doing everything in his power to get to the woman he loved.

After driving for what seemed like forever down a deserted road, Shaun finally pointed and said, "There!"

Cash's heart was in this throat when he spotted Imogen standing on the side of the road, waving wildly. He slammed on the brakes and stopped right next to her. Before either of them could say anything, Imogen yanked the back door open and hopped in.

"It's the house at the top of the hill. Go," Imogen ordered.

Shaun spun in his seat as Cash turned up the steep road. "What happened?"

"We were taking the Mustang for a spin before lunch, and it broke down here. Neither of us had cell service, so we hiked up to the house to see if they had a phone. No one was there, so I magicked my way in. The moment we were inside the house, Crazy Cora attacked. Harlow saved me from being possessed again, but she ended up taking my place instead. Now we need to save her."

"You're sure she's possessed?" Cash asked, knowing that sometimes it wasn't easy to tell depending on how the spirit handled themselves.

"I'm positive. Harlow isn't herself at all. Cash, she needs you."

The moment Cash pulled the Jeep to a stop in front of the house, he bolted from the driver's seat and grabbed his pack from the cargo area. Shaun was waiting for him a few feet away, but Imogen was nowhere to be seen.

"Imogen?" he called.

"I'm going for help. Take care of Harlow until I get back," Imogen called from the driver's seat and then sped away.

Cash stared at Shaun with a look of disbelief. "Do we still believe it's Harlow who's possessed?"

Shaun looked shaken. But then he steeled himself and said, "Yes, but there's only one way to find out."

The pair of them turned to the house. Cash handed Shaun a bag of salt and said, "Pour this around the house. A nice thick layer. It will keep the spirit trapped in the house while I deal with it."

"Okay. I'll be in to help as soon as it's done," Shaun said, taking the salt.

"No." Cash shook his head. "Stay out here. I'll come get you when I'm sure it's safe."

"Cash, I'm not just going to leave you alone to deal with a crazy spirit," Shaun insisted.

"You can and you will," Cash said, his tone final. Then he softened it and said, "Trust me, Shaun."

His brother shook his head, clearly wanting to argue, but when he met Cash's worried gaze, he relented. "Okay, but just know that if things get too bad, I'm not just going to stand around and wait for her to destroy you. You're the only family I've got."

"Understood." Cash gave him a quick hug and then ran into the house. He found Harlow lying across an oversize chair, her feet dangling over the armrest while she read some gossip magazine. The place was a mess with debris everywhere, glass and ceramic shards on the floor from picture frames and at least one lamp. "Harlow?"

"Cash, finally," she said, breathing out a sigh of relief. She uncurled from her position on the chair and stood gracefully, her chest lifted and her back arched, causing her booty to stick out further. "I was wondering what was taking you so long."

She strolled over to him, her body movements exaggerated in a seductive manner.

Cash had never seen Harlow move like that, ever. She was athletic and graceful and one hundred percent authentic. There wasn't a doubt in his mind that Shaun had been correct. Harlow had been possessed. He glanced around at the destruction. "Imogen said you were cleaning up in here."

She waved an unconcerned hand. "We can hire someone to do that. Let's just get out of here." Cora walked up to Cash and placed her hand on his chest. She looked up at him through lowered lashes and in a seductive voice said, "I have plans for you."

"Oh, yeah?" Cash said, trying to match her tone as he lightly wrapped his fingers around her wrist. "And what would that be exactly?"

Cora stared at his lips and then raked her gaze down his body.

The attention made his skin crawl. Even though she looked like Harlow, there was nothing about this person that embodied her.

"Let's just say that by the time I'm through with you, life will never be the same."

"I could say the same to you." He tightened his grip on her wrist and spun her around so that her arm was yanked up behind her and her back was to his chest. After wrapping his free arm around her neck in a chokehold, he whispered, "You can't fool me, Cora. Did you really think I wouldn't know?"

She let out a bark of laughter. "You're smarter than you look."

He rolled his eyes. When it came to villains, she was such a cliché. "Get ready to burn in hell."

"How are you going to send me there?" she asked conversationally as if she weren't trapped in his vicelike grip.

"Telling you would ruin the surprise," he grunted and then shoved her away just as he reached for his iron chain and lashed out. Before it could wrap around her, she sent a spark of magic toward it, but she missed. The chain wrapped around her, trapping her in place. "That wasn't so hard, was it?"

She scowled at him. "Now what? You and I both know you need Harlow to help you expel me. Since I have control over her, that's not going to happen. The only way to get rid of me is to kill me. And if you do that, no more Harlow. What's it gonna be, Cash? A life with a shell of your former love or no love at all?"

Cash itched to ring her neck, but she had a point. Anything he did to her would only hurt Harlow, and there was no way he'd ever do that.

"Exploit her weakness, Cash!" Cora shouted and then quickly clamped her mouth shut. Her face nearly turned purple with rage.

Ahh, that was Harlow. He'd know her anywhere and that meant she still had some autonomy. More than Imogen had when she was possessed. It strengthened his resolve to send Cora to hell where she belonged. If only Harlow had given him a hint as to what her weakness actually might be.

"I'm not weak," Cora said in an icy tone that sent a chill down Cash's spine. "In fact, I'm stronger than ever." She lifted one hand and touched the iron chain. Closing her eyes, she seemed to focus her will. Then without warning, smoke started to rise from where the chain was encircling her.

"What are you going to do, Cora? Go up in flames just to free yourself from the iron?"

"If I have to," she snarled.

"You'll kill yourself if you do that," he said with more confidence than he could currently muster. His worry for Harlow was at an all-time high. He knew just how crazy the spirit was, and if she chose to have a showdown with him, she was probably insane enough to risk losing Harlow's body just to win this battle.

"So? I won't be any worse off than I was an hour ago. Besides, that will just make it easier to claim Imogen. Harlow won't be around to stop it."

"But I will!" Cash yelled. "And so will my brother. If you think you're getting through us, think again."

"It's working right now." Harlow's clothes burst into flames, and Cash immediately released her and then tackled her to the floor to put out the fire. By the time the flames were extinguished, Cora was on her feet, cackling and heading for the door.

"Stop!" Cash demanded. "What do you want from me?"

She turned and slowly raised one eyebrow. "What makes you think I want something from you?"

"If you didn't, you wouldn't have waited around for me to arrive. You had to know what a risk that would be."

She nodded. "That's fair. Okay, there *is* something I want. And if you want Harlow to survive, you're going to give it to me."

"What's that?"

"Harlow's life. Hollywood. The money. The fame. I want it all. Get me a contract, and I'll keep your precious Harlow safe until I'm done with this body."

Cash felt ill. "And how long will that be?"

"Right about the time her star burns out in Hollywood. By then, I'll be ready for a new and improved body."

"Fame and fortune? That's it? You want the spotlight?" he

reiterated. "And in a few years, when Harlow's body isn't considered young enough anymore, you'll move on?"

"Yeah," she said, sounding pleased with herself. "You've got it now. I deserve to be running with the elite. It's in my bloodline."

Cash raised his eyebrows. "Were you royalty in your past life or something?"

Her lips formed a tight line. "Something like that."

"A lady in waiting?"

Her nostrils flared.

Cash had to fight to keep a self-satisfied smile off his face. That was it. He'd found her weakness. *Thank you, Harlow.* This woman would always be insecure, and this entire horrific event fed off her belief that she deserved better in life. "Let me guess, a certain king kept you as his side piece for years but married someone else?"

"Royalty has its own rules," she said tightly.

"You were a commoner and weren't good enough for him?" Cash guessed.

"No! I was titled. A lady, I'll have you know. There was no reason why he couldn't have married me. I'd have made a much better queen than that wet noodle of a woman. And I'd be the one in the history books as the one everyone adored. Not her."

Cash had no idea who she was talking about. He didn't even care. All he knew was that no one would have adored this selfish, trash human. But he was breaking her down. He could almost see her coming apart at the seams. "You think whatever deal I get for you will turn you into a star?"

"Yes," she said confidently.

"You do realize they'll want us both, right? The draw is our relationship, not necessarily our ghost-hunting skills."

"Hmm, I guess that's not a surprise, considering neither of you could banish me," she said with an air of pride.

"Are you prepared to be my lover for the next however many years? After all this time, there's no faking it for the cameras. The public will see right through that."

"Oh, now we're talking." She scanned his body and looked nearly feral doing it. "I could get used to a gorgeous piece of meat like you. This isn't scaring me off. It's sweetening the deal, Cash Moses."

Cash's stomach turned, but he had to see this through to the end. He reached up and pressed a palm to her cheek with one hand and pulled her into him with the other.

She caught her breath, waiting in anticipation.

He growled and then buried his hand in her hair and yanked it as hard as he could, bending her backward. "You'll never know my touch, you vapid piece of trash! No wonder your king wouldn't marry you. You're worthless. Definitely not crown material."

Her lips twisted into a snarl, and then three things happened at once. Cash yanked her back up onto her feet and spun her around so that she was facing away from him, just as Harlow's voice broke free, yelling, "*Libetas!*"

Meanwhile, the front door burst open and Imogen, Miranda Moon, and two other witches he didn't know filed in. All of them were holding white pillar candles and chanting something in Latin that Cash couldn't decipher.

When he turned back to Harlow, he saw her kneeling on the floor, gasping for air. And right in front of her was the outline of a spirit that he knew had to be Cora.

The witches that surrounded them chanted louder and louder and louder until the lights flickered in the house. Cora's outline rose into the middle of the circle, and suddenly she started screaming so loud Cash almost believed she might be a banshee.

And then suddenly, the spirit burst into a million pieces and faded into nothing.

"She's gone," Harlow said in a trembling voice. "For good."

Cash stumbled toward her, wrapping her in his arms as everyone else started to talk at once.

CHAPTER 26

"She's gone, right?" Shaun called as he rushed into the house. "I felt her leave. Tell me she's gone."

"She's gone," Imogen said, walking over to Shaun and burying herself in his arms.

Shaun's gaze found Harlow. "Are you all right?"

Harlow nodded, clutching Cash's hand with both of hers. He had one arm around her and had pulled her in so that she was leaning against him. "You felt her leave?"

He cleared his throat. "Yes. For days now, ever since I had that premonition that didn't come true, I've felt a little off. Almost like I was coming down with something. And today when I had my last premonition, I was almost feverish. But suddenly, right after I felt all that magic in the air, that uneasiness that I'd thought was just me feeling rundown lifted, and now I remember those visions completely differently."

Cash tightened his grip on Harlow and said, "I suspected she was manipulating your visions when they didn't come true."

Shaun stiffened. "How?"

"Who knows? How did she possess both Imogen and Harlow?" Cash asked.

"She was a very old, very powerful spirit," Harlow said, finally ready to take charge of the conversation. "Because we all have ties to Imogen, she was likely able to tap into us easier because she had a piece of Imogen's energy. Possession does that to a person."

"Oh, gods," Imogen said, burying her face in Shaun's shoulder. "I'm so sorry I brought her into your life."

"Don't be sorry," he whispered. "It wasn't your fault."

"He's right, Gen," Harlow said. "None of this is your fault. We all suffered from her selfishness." Harlow glanced around at the witches that Imogen brought with her and felt a sense of gratitude that made her soul ache. "How did you guys get here or know we needed help?"

Imogen cleared her throat. "After the night out on the golf carts, I got a sense of the Keating Hollow witches' considerable power and decided I couldn't leave your fate solely in Cash's hands. I knew I wouldn't know what to do to help, but I figured a witch who was a medium might have some answers, so I hightailed it to Keating Hollow Books and found Brinn. Once I explained what was happening, she insisted on helping, as did Miranda, who'd just stopped in to sign more books. And it was Brinn's idea to pick up Zya from the yarn shop since Brinn said she was the most powerful medium she knew. All of them acted without hesitation."

It was something Harlow would always be grateful for and would never forget. This was what life was all about. Family. Chosen family. This was her fortune. Not the dollars that were stashed away in a bank account. It was the people who would show up for each other when they were needed most. Tears stung her eyes. Brinn, Miranda, and Zya had been friends, though not particularly close friends since she'd moved to town, but Harlow was beginning to see that maybe that was her fault. These gorgeous, courageous women had come to her aid, no questions asked, and had helped save her and Imogen from a spirit that had been ruining their lives for well over a year.

Breaking away from Cash, Harlow hugged and thanked all three of them and then said, "You're family now. Just know that whatever you need, I'm here. No questions asked."

Miranda let out a small chuckle. "We already knew that, Harlow. The way you took care of everyone during the solstice, that's just who you are. We're fortunate to have you here in Keating Hollow."

Brinn and Zya both agreed and then the four of them shared a group hug while tears trickled down Harlow's cheeks. When she finally broke free, Imogen was there, thanking them and vowing to always be of help when they needed her.

"Well, I think our work here is done," Zya said with a cheeky grin. "We have two more witches in our arsenal who have pledged their lives to us. Come on, witches. It's time we go plan our world domination." She winked at Harlow and then all of them started to crack up. When they sobered, Zya said, "No, seriously. You two are part of our coven now. Meetings are Tuesday nights at six."

"You have coven meetings?" Harlow asked, not sure she wanted to devote one night a week to spell work.

"It's book club," Brinn said, rolling her eyes. "We have wine or cocktails and charcuterie. You should come. We'd love to have you." She turned to Imogen. "You, too. You're one of us now."

"I'm in," Imogen said immediately.

Harlow smiled at her sister. She'd closed herself off for so long, and now she was opening up and making friends. There was no way she'd miss book club. "I'll be there. Tell me what to bring."

"We'll add you to the group chat," Brinn said and squeezed her hand. "Ready ladies? I need to get back to the store."

The three witches said their goodbyes, leaving Shaun, Imogen, Cash, and Harlow in the unfamiliar house.

"You know what?" Harlow said.

"What, gorgeous?" Cash asked.

"Cora had one good idea. We should hire someone to clean this place up and find out who the owner is so we can let them know what's gone down."

"I'm sure Wanda can tell us," Imogen said.

Harlow nodded, more than ready for a hot bath and a giant glass of wine. "Good, we have a plan. Should we get out of here?"

"Definitely."

Once they were outside, Imogen went to use her magic to lock the door but then hesitated. "I don't think I can," she said, glancing around nervously.

"Sure you can," Harlow urged. "You unlocked it fine."

"But I also summoned Cora. What if she comes back?" Her face turned pale. "What if my magic summons some other ghost?"

"Cora is gone for good," Harlow said earnestly. "That spell you guys did, it was a permanent banishing. I felt it in my bones, Gen. I promise you. But if any other spirit shows up, which, let's face it, is always going to be a possibility when I'm around, we'll deal with it. I'm here. So are Shaun and Cash. We'll deal with it together."

Cash and Shaun, who were standing behind them, both murmured their agreement.

Imogen stood at the door, her hand shaking. But she was a Thane, and nothing kept the Thane girls down for long. After a moment, she touched the knob. The lock slid into place and then they all waited.

Nothing.

There were no spirits, nothing terrible had happened, and life as a witch had gone back to normal.

Imogen let out a relieved sigh. "Thank the gods." She gave Harlow a hug and then walked over to Shaun. The two of them linked their fingers and led the way to Cash's Jeep.

When they finally had cell reception again, Harlow called the tow truck for the Mustang, and then they stopped at her rental first. Shaun and Imogen disappeared into the house the moment Cash stopped the car.

Harlow chuckled as she watched them hurry inside. "They are *so* dating. I don't care what they say."

"No doubt about it," Cash agreed. "I think they both are afraid to define anything. But we know better. At this rate, we're gonna wake up and they'll have been together for two years, still telling us they're not serious."

Harlow laughed. "And what about us? Are we serious?"

"About as serious as a relationship can get," Cash said as he pulled the black velvet box out of his pocket. "I was going to wait longer to give this back to you, but after today, I just don't want to wait one more minute."

"Wait!" Harlow held her index finger up. "I need just one sec before you finish that sentence. Can you do that for me? Hold on while I run inside and get something?"

Cash frowned in confusion but nodded. "You're kind of putting a crimp in my speech, but sure. I can wait a moment."

"You won't regret it," Harlow said, flashing him a stunning smile. "I promise." She jumped out of the Jeep, ran into the house, packed a quick overnight bag, and then grabbed the cigar box that she kept on her dresser. When she returned to the SUV, she noted she'd only been gone for two minutes. "I'm ready now."

He chuckled. "I think maybe the moment has passed."

"The hell it has," she said, turning to him. "Break out that velvet box, buddy."

Cash opened his hand, revealing he'd been holding it the entire time. "Harlow Thane, the last time I proposed to you it was in a car. If that car wasn't being towed to the repair shop as we speak, I'd have asked you for the second time in the car we love so much. But since I can't, my Jeep will have to do."

Harlow let out a small huff of laughter. "Seems fitting after all that's happened."

"It does, doesn't it?" His eyes glinted as he opened the velvet box, revealing the perfect ring, the one she'd worn for nearly eight months before she'd given it back to him last year. "Harlow Thane, will you marry me. Be my partner, wife, and best friend for the rest of our days?"

Harlow's heart was ready to burst. Before she answered with a resounding yes, she opened the cigar box and pulled out the small pouch that housed the ring she'd had made for him just before everything went to hell last year. She held it out and said, "I will if you will."

Cash took the platinum ring and read the inscribed quote out loud. "*All of our days and nights.*" His eyes turned misty. It was the quote he always used to say to her when he told her he loved her. "Hell yes, gorgeous," he said, wiping the tears from his eyes. "I love you. And I always will for all of my days and nights."

"Good." She slipped her diamond ring on her finger, leaned

over, and said, "That's never coming off this time. No matter what. That's a promise."

"I'm going to hold you to that," he said, his voice hoarse with emotion.

"You better."

Cash pulled her into his arms and kissed her like he was a starving man. When he finally pulled away, Harlow said, "Let's get moving. I have plans for you."

His eyes glinted with mischief as he slammed the Jeep into gear and sped all the way home.

CHAPTER 27

*A*bout a week after they banished Cora for good, Harlow pulled into the driveway of her rental and laid into the horn. When her sister didn't appear right away, she laid into it again, this time holding it down longer just to be obnoxious. There was no way Imogen hadn't heard the horn the first time.

The door swung open, and Imogen stomped out, still trying to get her sweater on. "Chill out, would you? You're gonna wake the gnomes."

Harlow chuckled and leaned back in her seat, feeling better than she had in... well, over a year. It looked like Imogen did too, because she was simply glowing when she slipped into the Subaru.

"Okay, I'm here. Where's the fire?" she asked as she fastened her seatbelt.

"Downtown. There's somewhere we need to be in about ten minutes. Ready?"

"I'm not sure. If I say yes, what am I agreeing to?" Imogen asked, casting her sister a suspicious look.

"I can't tell you. It's a surprise."

Imogen groaned. "This isn't going to be like that surprise birthday party you threw for me when no one showed up, is it?"

Harlow winced. That had been an epic failure. All Harlow wanted to do was give her sister the best sweet-sixteen party a girl could ask for. Unfortunately, she'd scheduled it the same night as an epic rainstorm that shut down streets and caused major power outages. They'd been stuck eating cake for days. "Listen, I can't be held responsible for what mother nature does."

"The news had been warning it was coming for almost two weeks!"

"Yeah, fair point. I should have rescheduled, but I was young and dumb then. I'm much smarter now. Trust me. You're gonna love it."

Imogen gave her a skeptical look. "We'll see."

Harlow laughed and so did Imogen. It felt good to laugh with her sister again. Harlow had missed that almost more than anything.

Five minutes later, they pulled into a parking spot on Main Street next to a metallic green Jeep.

"That's gorgeous," Imogen said, admiring it. "Look at that finish. It's the perfect model, too. Jeep Wrangler with a hardtop. Lucky bastard."

"Come on," Harlow said, climbing out of her Subaru. The Mustang was still at the shop. It turned out not only had it had a belt issue, but it had a transmission issue as well, and they were still waiting on the parts. Since they'd already agreed that Harlow was taking the Mustang back, Harlow was paying for the repairs and wasn't in a real hurry to get it back. She just wanted it done right this time. She didn't relish being stranded on a lonely road out in the middle of the woods. Not again.

Imogen followed Harlow onto the cobbled sidewalk, but when Harlow didn't lead her anywhere, she said, "Well? Now where? And can we make a stop at Incantation Café? I could really use a piece of coffee cake. The pickins are slim at chez Thane."

"Really? Why? Won't Shaun take you to the store to get provisions?"

Her face flushed pink as she glanced away and mumbled something Harlow couldn't hear.

"What was that?"

She cleared her throat. "We were going to go last night, but we got a little distracted."

"I see." Harlow let out a bark of laughter. "The honeymoon period is so intense."

"We're not in our honeymoon period," she said, rolling her eyes. "We're just seeing where things go."

"Uh-huh. Just seeing where things go while he straight-up moves in. Sounds like a serious relationship to me."

"He hasn't moved in," Imogen insisted. "He's just giving you and Cash space."

"Sure. Space," Harlow said with a snicker. The day after she and Cash got re-engaged, they'd made the decision that she'd move into Aunt Jane's house. And Harlow had told Imogen to stay at the rental for as long as she wanted since there was a two-year lease. Imogen had protested, but Harlow insisted, telling her she could start paying rent when her business was stable enough for her to draw an appropriate salary.

Imogen had finally accepted but insisted she'd pay her back. Harlow told her she'd just put it in a high yield savings account in Imogen's name, so why bother. The argument had ended there, and Harlow packed her stuff and moved. So far the arrangement was working perfectly. Aunt Jane was happy and had taken to baking yummy treats every few days for them. Shaun only came back to the house to help Cash when he needed him for the remodel, and they'd instituted a weekly Sunday brunch for the four of them to get together. Everything was just about perfect.

Almost.

"Can we eat now?" Imogen asked.

"Sure." Harlow walked toward the two empty store spaces right in front of them and produced a set of keys. "Just as soon as we see our new offices."

Imogen blinked at her. "Excuse me?"

Harlow grinned as she unlocked the door on the right. "Which one do you want? The one on the left or the right? I was thinking maybe the right since the floral shop is right next door. But the left is closer to Incantation Café, so it's a toss-up, really."

"Harlow!" Imogen said with an incredulous laugh. "What in the world is going on?"

"Let's see." Harlow waved her into the office and said, "Why don't you sit down."

Imogen glanced around at the empty space and said, "Where?"

"Behind the counter," Harlow said and went to lean against what must have previously been a checkout counter but could easily be a receptionist's desk or a place to hold sample albums or wedding magazines.

Imogen tentatively moved behind the counter and chuckled when she saw one of the stools from her kitchen. "When did you get this out of the house?"

"Mind your business," Harlow said with a wink. "Tell me

what you think. I was talking to Chad a few days ago, and he mentioned that these two spaces were up for rent. And because they are relatively small, they are dirt cheap. Most people around here who want a store on Main Street need square footage. But we don't. Basically we just need offices. The rent is cheaper if I lease both, and then I get to decide who I want as a neighbor instead of being stuck with someone who smokes outside my door all day."

"I'm sorry," Imogen said. "But why do you need office space?"

This was the part that Harlow had been dreading. She'd hoped the excitement of an office space on Main Street would take the sting out of what Harlow had to tell her sister. "Okay, just hear me out before you say anything, all right?"

"I'm listening," Imogen said, sounding impatient.

Harlow couldn't blame her. She was acting like a manic idiot. She'd just been so nervous she hadn't known how to handle it. "Cash and I were talking, and we'd like to work part time, very part time, as ghost hunters."

Imogen's eyes darkened and Harlow could already see her shutting down.

"Not like we did before. Just listen, okay?"

"I'm still listening."

"Right. Well, after you were possessed and then I went through the same thing, I just feel like there needs to be somewhere that people who are dealing with rogue ghosts can go for help. I don't want to invite trouble like we used to with our show. I mean, I'm not going to go into old places and asks ghosts to show themselves, but when someone is being haunted or harassed by a stubborn ghost, Cash and I want to help. I figured if we opened a ghost-hunting office and only worked with private clients by appointment, that would satisfy our needs of being available when people need us. But I really, *really* don't want to invite anyone who is haunted into the house. So this was the solution." Harlow gave her a nervous grimace. "What do you think?"

Imogen just stared at her with her mouth hanging open.

Harlow's stomach sank. She felt strongly about this, but she didn't want to do anything to ruin her relationship with her sister. She didn't know what she'd do if Imogen hated it. Couldn't she see that Harlow and Cash just wanted to help?

"Harlow," Imogen finally said, her voice a little hoarse with emotion. "I think that everything you said was just wonderful. Of course you should use your gifts to help people." Her expression softened. "I know I put you through hell last year, but that was about me and my fears. Not you or how much I trust you."

"I have a confession to make too," Harlow admitted.

"About what?" Imogen frowned.

"My year off from ghost hunting and my breakup with Cash. I didn't just do it for you. I did it for me, too."

"I don't understand," Imogen said, her face pinched with worry. "What does that mean?"

Harlow let out a sigh and owned up to the truth she'd always known but hadn't been able to put into words before now. "When you were possessed, it shook me to my core. And when I almost lost you? Well, that was all I could see in my dreams for months. I didn't want anything to do with ghost hunting after that. And that's why I went scorched earth. I was scared. But then I didn't have Cash. I didn't have you. And ghosts were popping up anyway. My plans to stay away from them were futile and then… You know the rest. It's time for me to go back to what I was meant to do and pray that the people I love are okay with it."

"I'm okay with it," Imogen said. "I promise."

"You really don't mind?" Harlow asked, praying she hadn't misunderstood.

"No. This is what you were born for, and we've both already seen that even when you try to ignore your gift it finds you anyway. Running is a fool's errand." She reached out and squeezed her sister's hands. "Just be careful, okay? Because even though I think it's a good idea for you, I'd rather stick to weddings."

"In an office space right next to mine?" Harlow asked hopefully.

"You're too much. You know that, right? You already pay my housing rent. I can't let you pay my office space rent, too."

"Sure you can. It's really not that much more for the second office, so I'm taking it either way. I just hope I get to see a friendly face next door when I'm in there working. If not paying rent bothers you, you can take over the cleaning duties. Especially those front windows. They need a good scrubbing before we set out window displays."

Imogen glanced around the room, really studying it. "It would be a great space for picking fabrics and florals. That front window really lets in a lot of light."

"So you're in?" Harlow asked.

"I'm in. And I'll wash the windows. Just stop paying for things for me. You're making me feel like a socialite."

Harlow winced. "Um, how about just *one* more thing, and then I'm done."

Imogen shook her head. "Harlow, I don't need anything else besides a car, but—"

Harlow held up a key fob and handed it to her sister. "I know I didn't take you with me to look at it, but I think you're going to like it anyway."

Imogen followed Harlow's gaze to the green Jeep Wrangler that was parked next to the Subaru. "You didn't," she whispered.

"I did," Harlow whispered back.

Imogen pressed the Unlock button and watched as the lights on the Jeep flashed. She let out a squeal and then wrapped her sister in a bear hug. "You're too much," Imogen said into her ear.

"Probably, but I also have far too much just because I was on a television show. Sharing with the person I love most in the world just seems like the right thing to do."

"So with Cash?" Imogen teased.

"Ha-ha. Cash has his own money. He can fend for himself. You, however, are rebuilding your life, and I want nothing more than to help you do that. Just say yes, Gen. It's not your fault your life was ruined by that ghost. Let me help lift you back up."

Imogen's chin quivered, and tears stood in her eyes. "It was never your responsibility to do that, Harlow." There was no heat or judgment in her tone. Just resignation laced with emotion. "I don't deserve you after the way I treated you."

Harlow's heart squeezed, and she nearly thought she'd pass out from the pressure. But when Imogen's arms came around her, suddenly the world was right again. She had Cash, her sister, and a new storefront that would put her in a position to help people in need.

It was all she'd ever wanted.

CHAPTER 28

*S*adie Lewis grabbed a beer mug, and before she could get it under the tab, the glass slipped from her hand and shattered on the cement floor. She bit back the curse that was on the tip of her tongue and turned to the customer. "I'm so sorry about that. Let me just sweep this up real quick, and then I'll get that beer for you."

"No problem," the handsome man said, looking more amused than annoyed.

Of course he found it funny. He wasn't the one who had to clean up shards of glass.

The door swung open, and another group of people walked in, making the knots tighten in her gut. Why tonight, of all nights, did half the town have to show up?

"Sadie! Great turn out tonight!" Imogen Thane called from across the room and gave her two thumbs-up when she caught Sadie's eye. She was sitting with her sister, Harlow, and their significant others. After working with Imogen on her cousin's wedding the two had become pretty good friends. The kind of friends who showed up to support each other, apparently. Much to Sadie's chagrin.

Sadie waved, both grateful for and annoyed by her friend's support. Didn't she understand that the more people who were in the audience tonight, the more nervous Sadie was going to be?

No, Sadie, she doesn't because you never told her that, Sadie chided herself.

"Your friend's right. It's a good turnout tonight," the handsome stranger said, watching her. "Is it always this busy in here?"

Sadie continued to sweep up the glass and only briefly glanced at him. "It can be. The Keating Hollow Brewery is an award-winning pub. Most people who visit town usually end up here eventually."

"If the beers are as interesting as the staff, then I can see why," he said with a sexy little half grin.

Okay, that was nice. It wasn't every day that Sadie was hit on. But that probably had more to do with the fact that most of her customers were married than anything else. Keating Hollow seemed to be a commitment town, and the pool of dateable men in her age range was pretty slim. Most of her matches on dating apps came from men thirty to fifty miles away. Not that they'd proved to be winners, obviously. Otherwise, she'd have given up the dating app. But this guy? He had potential.

Once she was done sweeping and washing her hands, she quickly got on that beer she owed the hottie. Then she said, "Sorry about the wait. Can I get you a complimentary appetizer?" That's right. Sadie Lewis wasn't above bribing cute men to like her.

"Complimentary, huh? Well, I would be foolish to turn that down." He quickly scanned the menu. "The crab dip looks interesting."

"Crab dip it is," she said and sent him a wink of her own. As she tapped it into the ordering system she asked, "What brings you to Keating Hollow?"

"I just needed a change of pace. I have a friend who lives here who said I could use his house, so here I am. So far I'd say it was an excellent decision." The way he was eyeing her, there was no missing his innuendo. "And you? You obviously work here, but did you grow up here or are you a transplant?"

"Born and bred," she said and poured another beer. "Keating Hollow might seem a little on the tame side, but it's a gorgeous place full of fantastic people. I hope you enjoy it while you're here."

"I will… if you agree to let me take you out," he said, eyeing her with a cocky smile.

Sadie couldn't help it. She laughed. "I bet that always works for you. I bet that every time you've asked someone out like that, they've eaten it right up."

He shrugged one shoulder. "I do okay in the dating department."

"I bet. When you look like that, it's hard to strike out."

It was his turn to laugh. "You think you have me all figured out, don't you?"

"Maybe not *all* figured out. Let me guess. You're a D-list actor who's desperately trying to raise your star in the business and you're here to woo Miranda and Cameron so you can get a part in their next project."

"D-list? Ouch." He clutched his chest as if she'd shot him. "You wound me. But no. Not an actor. Try again."

"Not an actor. Okay, a reality star? Something like *Love in the Redwoods*," she tried again. The man had a polish about him that just screamed Hollywood. And if he had a friend who had a house he could borrow, it wasn't out of the realm of possibility. A lot of stars ended up in Keating Hollow at one point or another.

That made him laugh out loud. "Definitely not a reality star. What else do you have?"

"Trust fund kid?"

"Far from it," he said and took a sip of his beer.

"Sadie?" Clay, the brewery manager, called from the other end of the bar. "Are you ready for your break?"

"Sure, boss." She looked at her customer. "Need anything before I head out for a few minutes?"

"Your number." He held out his phone for her to type it in.

Sadie's lips twitched with amusement. Normally she didn't really go for cocky guys, but this one had a charm that she just couldn't seem to resist. She gave him a hint of a smile and then tapped in her number.

The moment he took his phone back, he hit the number. When her phone started to ring from her back pocket, he grinned. "Just checking. Enjoy your break, Sadie."

She rolled her eyes at him, but as she walked away, she couldn't help looking over her shoulder at the man with the dark blue eyes and dark curly hair. He tilted his head toward the door, silently asking if she wanted to join him.

Why the hell not? she asked herself. She was twenty-seven years old and deserved to enjoy a handsome stranger for the night, right? With a short nod, she reversed course and followed him out front. The moment she was free of the pub, he tucked her hand in his and led her down the cobblestone sidewalk until they were standing in front of A Spoonful of Magic's magical window. It was enchanted to show chocolate bunnies playing leapfrog with the yellow marshmallow ducks. Gumdrops had been utilized to look like a rainbow river, and everything about it screamed happiness and joy.

"What's your name?" Sadie asked him.

He gave her a wry smile. "You gave your number to a complete stranger. I thought that was frowned upon, even in small towns."

She shrugged one shoulder. "Once you give me your name, we'll no longer be strangers, right?"

He chuckled. "It's King."

"Oh, so not Hollywood. You're royalty. How pretentious of you," she joked.

He snorted. "Hardly. I think my mom just wanted to pretend we were something more than we were. It's harmless, but I'm about as far away from the crown as one can get."

"You gotta give her points for originality, I suppose," Sadie said.

He smiled down at her. "Maybe."

After a few beats of silence, Sadie said, "I've always loved this store. The window displays usually change each month, and the owner, Miss Maple, is just about the kindest person I've ever met."

"This is what I came here for," he said wistfully.

"Chocolate? It's good, but I'm not sure it was worth traveling for."

"No, Sadie of Keating Hollow. I meant the small-town flavor. You don't get this where I'm from. Not even close."

Sadie tilted her head to look up at him. "I'm getting the feeling that my first impressions of you were way off."

"You could say that," he said with a wry smile.

She nodded. "Okay. I'm intrigued."

"Good." He gave her that sexy half smile. "What time do you get off?"

"Tonight? Nine o'clock."

"I'll be here." Then he walked off in the opposite direction of the brewery, leaving her at the window. Sadie shook her head, wondering what in the world that was about, and then she went back to work, grateful for the short distraction.

An hour later, Abby Garrison got up on the small stage in the brewery and said, "Good evening, everyone. We have a special treat for you tonight. Are you ready for some really excellent music?"

A deafening cheer filled the bar, and Abby beamed.

"Wonderful. Well, let me introduce Austin Steele, Keating Hollow's very own resident music producer. Give it up for Austin."

Everyone cheered while his wife Brinn let out a loud whistle.

Sadie remained a ball of nerves. Tonight was the night she was supposed to get up there and sing. It was her official audition to be signed to Austin's label. She just didn't know when it was going to happen. Right now? Later? She wished her nerves would settle. Otherwise, she was going to lose her lunch right along with her courage.

Austin came up on stage. "I'll make it short and sweet. Tonight we have a special guest. Put your hands together for King McGrath."

The band started to play and instantly, Sadie recognized the song. It had been a popular hit a few years back. "Small Town Love." It was catchy but a little too pop for her taste. And that's when it hit her that the guy she'd met was the pop star King

McGrath. He strode out onto the stage with his guitar, already strumming it. Then he spoke into the microphone and said, "We have another surprise for you tonight. Sadie Lewis? Can you come up here?"

She stood there frozen like a deer in the headlights. When Austin had said he wanted her to sing tonight as part of her audition, he hadn't said anything about singing with a pop star.

"Sadie?" King's eyes met hers, and suddenly she found herself walking up to the stage and standing right next to the handsome man she'd been flirting with half the night.

He strummed the guitar and said, "Do you know this one?"

She nodded.

"Okay, you come in on the second verse." He winked, clearly trying to set her at ease.

Had he known all along she was a singer? Was that why he'd taken an interest in her? She wasn't going to find out right now. She had a song to sing.

"Bright lights in the rearview," he started. "Life has never been the same after you. Searching for something greater than that night beneath the northern lights."

Sadie felt the song come alive in her body and sang, "Looking back, you were worth the fight, my solace, my light. I'd give anything to lie with you under those northern lights."

The guitar strumming stopped abruptly, and King stared at her with a mix of wonder and pure contempt. Then he said, "It's you."

She blinked at him. "Excuse me?"

King glared at her and then, without a word, he stormed off the stage, leaving her in front of an entire restaurant full of people, all of them just as dumbfounded as she was.

Austin appeared and handed her a guitar. "Sing something. Anything." Then he bolted after his musician.

Sadie cleared her throat and then finished King's song. When she was done, she walked off the stage to varying degrees of applause and went to look for King and find out what happened. But he was gone, and there was a text on her phone from his number.

I'm the one leaving this time.

DEANNA'S BOOK LIST

Witches of Keating Hollow:
Soul of the Witch
Heart of the Witch
Spirit of the Witch
Dreams of the Witch
Courage of the Witch
Love of the Witch
Power of the Witch
Essence of the Witch
Muse of the Witch
Vision of the Witch
Waking of the Witch
Honor of the Witch
Promise of the Witch
Return of the Witch
Fortune of the Witch
Song of the Witch

Witches of Befana Bay:

The Witch's Silver Lining
The Witch's Secret Love

Witches of Christmas Grove:
A Witch For Mr. Holiday
A Witch For Mr. Christmas
A Witch For Mr. Winter
A Witch For Mr. Mistletoe
A Witch For Mr. Frost
A Witch For Mr. Garland

Premonition Pointe Novels:
Witching For Grace
Witching For Hope
Witching For Joy
Witching For Clarity
Witching For Moxie
Witching For Kismet

Miss Matched Midlife Dating Agency:
Star-crossed Witch
Honor-bound Witch
Outmatched Witch
Moonstruck Witch
Rainmaker Witch

Jade Calhoun Novels:
Haunted on Bourbon Street
Witches of Bourbon Street
Demons of Bourbon Street
Angels of Bourbon Street
Shadows of Bourbon Street

Incubus of Bourbon Street
Bewitched on Bourbon Street
Hexed on Bourbon Street
Dragons of Bourbon Street

Pyper Rayne Novels:
Spirits, Stilettos, and a Silver Bustier
Spirits, Rock Stars, and a Midnight Chocolate Bar
Spirits, Beignets, and a Bayou Biker Gang
Spirits, Diamonds, and a Drive-thru Daiquiri Stand
Spirits, Spells, and Wedding Bells

Ida May Chronicles:
Witched To Death
Witch, Please
Stop Your Witchin'

Crescent City Fae Novels:
Influential Magic
Irresistible Magic
Intoxicating Magic

Last Witch Standing:
Bewitched by Moonlight
Soulless at Sunset
Bloodlust By Midnight
Bitten At Daybreak

Witch Island Brides:
The Wolf's New Year Bride
The Vampire's Last Dance
The Warlock's Enchanted Kiss

The Shifter's First Bite

Destiny Novels:
Defining Destiny
Accepting Fate

Wolves of the Rising Sun:
Jace
Aiden
Luc
Craved
Silas
Darien
Wren

Black Bear Outlaws:
Cyrus
Chase
Cole

Bayou Springs Alien Mail Order Brides:
Zeke
Gunn
Echo

ABOUT THE AUTHOR

New York Times and USA Today bestselling author, Deanna Chase, is a native Californian, transplanted to the slower paced lifestyle of southeastern Louisiana. When she isn't writing, she is often goofing off with her husband in New Orleans or playing with her two shih tzu dogs. For more information and updates on newest releases visit her website at deannachase.com.